Calvin

Calvin

A NOVEL BY
Martine Leavitt

Margaret Ferguson Books
FARRAR STRAUS GIROUX
New York

Farrar Straus Giroux Books for Young Readers
175 Fifth Avenue, New York 10010

macteenbooks.com

Library of Congress Cataloging-in-Publication Data
Leavitt, Martine, 1953– author.
  Calvin / Martine Leavitt. — First edition.
    pages cm
  Summary: Born on the day the last Calvin and Hobbes comic strip was published, seventeen-year-old Calvin, a schizophrenic, sees and has conversations with the tiger, Hobbes, and believes that if he can persuade the strip's creator, Bill Watterson, to do one more strip, he will make Calvin well.
  ISBN 978-0-374-38073-1 (hardback)
  [1. Schizophrenia—Fiction. 2. Mental illness—Fiction. 3. High schools—Fiction. 4. Schools—Fiction. 5. Characters in literature—Fiction.] I. Title.

PZ7.B3217Cal 2015
[Fic]—dc23

                                                              2015002574

Our books may be purchased in bulk for promotional, educational, or business use. Please contact your local bookseller or the Macmillan Corporate and Premium Sales Department at (800) 221-7945 ext. 5442 or by e-mail at MacmillanSpecialMarkets@macmillan.com.

For Kevin, James, and Nicole

Calvin

"   "
— Mabel Syrup, author of *Hamster Huey and the Gooey Kablooie* and *Commander Coriander Salamander and 'Er Singlehander Bellylander*

"Where there is a work of art, there is no madness."
— Michel Foucault

"Children's book authors should be forced to read their stories aloud every single night of their rotten lives."
—Calvin's dad, in Bill Watterson, *Homicidal Psycho Jungle Cat: A Calvin and Hobbes Collection*

DEAR BILL,

This is Calvin again. I hope it's okay if I call you Bill. Meaning no disrespect at all, but Bill is easier to type than Mr. Watterson and this is going to be a long letter.

I am writing this letter for two reasons. One is because it has to be my English project, which is worth 50 percent of my final grade. My teacher gave me the idea but said it better be a long letter if it's going to be worth 50 percent.

So where do I start? They say a person my age knows maybe thirty thousand words, so picking the first word out of thirty thousand is the hardest part. After you pick the first word, it weirdly picks the next one, and that one picks the one after that, and next thing you know you're not in control at all—the pen is as big as a telephone pole and you're just hanging on for dear life—

Sometimes I riff like that. Sorry.

Everything I'm going to say in this letter is true with some real stuff thrown in. You may wonder how you can believe that, coming from a recently diagnosed schizo kid, but

I've figured out there's a difference between the meaning of the word *real* and the meaning of the word *true*. Reality is all the stuff that won't go away, like school and gravity, no matter how much you wish it would. It's the ceiling your imagination bumps up against. People with my condition just keep floating on up as if there weren't any ceiling, with every so often a few hard falls and then more floating.

But true doesn't float. It just is.

So this is how it started, Bill: I got sick.

It was Thursday night and that meant the next day was Friday, the day my English and biology projects were due. The English project was worth 50 percent of my final grade, and the science project was worth 40 percent.

I'd done a little research for biology.

I hadn't even started the English project.

Some people destroy their lives with addictive substances. I had just destroyed mine by procrastination. It was the end of January and the end of the first semester of my senior year. My parents were so proud of me because my grades were decent enough that they were sure I was headed to a good university to study neuroscience. Instead I was about to flunk English and biology, which would be black marks on my transcript forever, keeping me out of college and following me around like a virtual dunce cap for the rest of my life.

I was lying in bed thinking about this when the room started swelling and shrinking. I could feel it swelling and shrinking, and I was huge and small right along with my room, like I was Alice in Wonderland, like my body was a balloon and somebody was blowing me up and deflating me over and over again.

I was like, *what the heck*.

And then I heard a voice.

Hobbes: It's me.

I knew it was Hobbes. I knew right away it was him even though I couldn't see him.

Hobbes: It's me, Hobbes.

So, Bill, you know how when Calvin comes home from school every day and Hobbes knocks him off his feet at the door and his shoes go flying and stars and dust fly and moons and planets circle his head? That's how I felt when Hobbes started talking to me. In a voice I could hear. Knocked off my feet, shoes flying, little ringed planets over my head.

It had never been like that when I was a kid. When I was a kid, I decided what my Hobbes doll said. Sometimes I surprised myself by what I made him say, so it turned out almost like a real conversation between Calvin-me and Hobbes-me. Sometimes I forgot they were both me.

But this was different. This was a full-on voice that didn't seem to have anything to do with me.

I didn't answer him at first. I wasn't crazy: I knew he wasn't there. But he was. I could feel him, hear him breathing somewhere in my room.

Hobbes: I'm here. You just can't see me. Yet.

And, Bill, you know how when Calvin was mad or scared

and his face would turn into this big black hole with a pink tongue in the middle? That's how I felt when Hobbes kept talking to me. So I just lay there in bed with my black-hole head and my pink tongue in the middle of it for a long time.

Then it went like this:

Me (whispering): I'm too old for an imaginary friend.

Hobbes: I'm not imaginary.

Me: Yes, you are.

Hobbes: I'm real.

Me: No.

Hobbes: Okay. I'm true.

Me: Imaginary.

Hobbes: Okay. If I'm your imagination, make me say something.

Me: Say, tigers are doofuses.

I concentrated, trying to make him say it, but he didn't.

Hobbes: Nice try. You know my loyalty to cat-kind.

Me: Say it! This is my mind, and you are a product of my imagination, and if I tell you to say tigers are doofuses then you have to say it.

Hobbes:

Me: *Say it!*

Hobbes: Humans are doofuses.

Me: I'm telling Mom.

Hobbes: What are you going to tell her? That at age seventeen you have a man-eating tiger for an imaginary friend?

Me: Yes! Mo-om!

Hobbes: And you know what she's going to do? Take you to the doctor.

Me: Yeah. As she should.

Hobbes: And you know what the doctors are going to do to you?

Me:

Hobbes: Yes. Exactly.

Me: You were never real. I invented you, I can un-invent you.

Hobbes: Bill invented me.

Me: Okay, but I'm the one hearing you. I can stop hearing you.

Hobbes: Can you?

Me: Yeah. I can.

Hobbes: Try.

Me:

Hobbes: Are you trying?

Me:

Hobbes: I'm still here. You can ignore me all you want, it won't make me go away.

Me: You're just—you were just a toy—

Hobbes: That was then. You still trying?

Me: I'll keep on trying until you go away.

Hobbes: If you have to try to make something in your imagination go away, that means you are acknowledging it exists even as you are trying to pretend it doesn't. As soon as you wonder if you've made me go away, you're thinking about me again, and there I am. Whenever you think of me to wonder if I'm gone, I'm there, I'm here.

Just then Mom opened the door.

Mom: Calvin, did you call me?

Me: Yes—no—I must have been dreaming . . . Sorry.

Mom: Okay. Good night, son.

Me: Do you see Hobbes in here, Mom?

Mom: You *are* dreaming. We lost Hobbes a long time ago.

Hobbes: *Lost* is a euphemism. She washed me to death.

Mom: You okay, honey?

Me: Yeah.

Mom: Anything you want to talk about?

Me: No. Thanks, Mom. I'm going back to sleep now.

She shut the door.

Hobbes: You always were a smart kid.

WHEN I WAS NINE OR SO, MOM WASHED HOBBES TO death. She threw him into the washing machine with a few towels like she'd done lots of times before, but this time he busted up in there. When the wash was over, the towels were gummed up with tiger guts and tiger fur. Mom slowly pulled the mess out and into a basket, saying they were old towels anyway and maybe she'd just chuck the whole thing into the garbage and sorry, Calvin, I guess he just wore out.

Before Hobbes died I was one way, and after, I was different.

Before Hobbes died I wanted to win the Change the World Lottery. I wanted to be that person who does one thing that makes the world better. The world only spits up one of them every hundred years or so, and the odds were six billion to one that I'd win. Einstein won it with the theory of relativity, but given the lower population of the world, the odds when he was alive were slightly higher.

Before Hobbes died, I thought I could win that lottery. After Hobbes died, I started to see how dumb that was. I realized you have to be a freak of nature to win that lottery, I mean to really win. I wondered if it was worth it. Freakdom is a high price to pay for a ticket. I also began to wonder why I wanted to Change the World in the first place. Fame? Money? Was that any reason to want to Change the World?

Before Hobbes died, a cardboard box could be a time travel machine or a transmogrifier. After, it was just a cardboard box.

I noticed other things, too. After Hobbes died, I got scared of careening down steep hills in my wagon and on my sled. After Hobbes died, I wasn't scared of the monsters under the bed anymore. I started to be afraid of climate change and nuclear bombs and all the things I heard on the news that didn't go shrinking away when you turned on the light or your mom walked into the room.

Now I was seventeen and a tiger was talking to me and I wasn't scared of the monsters under the bed. I was scared of the monster *in* the bed, which was me.

It took a while, but somehow I fell asleep that night.

The next morning I stepped out of bed and fell to my death and found out why people scream on their way down.

Then I woke up for real and put my feet on the floor and fell to my death and found out that even when you've done it before you still scream on the way down.

Mom yelled through the door.

Mom: Calvin, what's going on? I called you three times. Hurry, you're going to be late!

So I got out of bed and I could see atoms. No, for real. I could see all the atoms that make up the world, and when I stood on the floor it was like a trillion billion ball bearings were under my feet.

I showered and felt hydrogen and oxygen hitting in alternate streams of molecules and when I sat down to shovel in scrambled eggs I could almost hear the baby chicken atoms saying don't eat me, but I ate them anyway and left for the bus.

Waiting with me at the bus stop in the rain, just out of my line of vision, was my buddy the man-eating tiger, Hobbes.

It was freaky in one way to have Hobbes there, but in another way it wasn't horrible. Since my only friend, Susie, had made new friends, I hadn't had anyone to hang out with for a long time. Now I had somebody to talk to, even if it was an imaginary tiger.

Hobbes started talking again clear as could be.

Hobbes: Lemme tell you what it was like to be washed to death. First you get a hole in you, and your guts start stretching out of you, and the hole gets bigger and the guts get longer, and soon you're swirling in soapy water and your own guts and fur, and you turn inside out, and your eyeballs sink to the bottom of the washing machine, each eyeball all alone, and you can't even see your other eyeball. And that's it until your best friend is laughing at your lonely eyeballs.

Me: It did look kind of funny.

It had, but I'd still been pretty choked up about it at the time.

Hobbes: I think you should make it up to me. Skip school. Let's play!

Me: Go away.

Hobbes: C'mon, buddy. We had good times. We will again. All the sled rides and the snowmen and the snowball fights and the forts.

Me: Remember I broke my arm *and* my leg last time we went sledding?

Hobbes: Remember all the adventures?

Me: All the fights.

Hobbes: All the exploring and climbing trees?

Me: All the trouble we got into.

Hobbes: Let's run away.

Me: People will think I'm insane because you talk to me.

Hobbes: Since when did we care what people think?

Me: There's more of them. The definition of sanity is a democratic thing. They get to decide.

Hobbes: We'll have our own reality.

Me: You can't have a reality all by yourself.

Hobbes: Why not?

Me: Because . . . because it's like playing Calvinball. If you make up the rules as you go, nobody else gets it, nobody else can play with you, you never know when the game is over or if you won . . . It's sort of pointless. And lonely.

Hobbes: You gave up on trying to win the Change the World Lottery.

Me: I could never win.

Hobbes: You should never give up on that.

Me: It's too hard. Besides, now I have to figure out how to deal with my problem.

Hobbes: What problem?

Me: You. You are my problem.

Hobbes: Your imagination is a transmogrifier.

Me: The transmogrifier was just a cardboard box. I want you to leave me alone. Go away.

Hobbes: No.

Me: I made you up. I can make you go away.

But he didn't go away, Bill. He stayed.

SCHOOL'S ALWAYS BEEN PRETTY BAD. MOM SAID THEY
were going to keep me back at the end of first grade, but
when they tested me they found out I was in the ninety-
sixth percentile for intelligence and they figured I was just
bored. Dad gave me lectures explaining how all the brains
in the world wouldn't do me any good if I didn't know how
to work. But as it turns out, all the lectures in the world
don't make things any less boring, and they don't make you
work harder either. So I aced classes where all I had to do
was show up and take tests. I didn't do as well in classes that
required projects.

It always bugged me that I went to school but I didn't
seem to learn anything really useful. Like birds. I saw the
same kinds of birds every day and there I was in my last year
of high school and I didn't know what kinds they were. Except robins. Shouldn't there be a class called Basic Birds?
What about flowers? Shouldn't there be a course called
Common Flowers You Will See in Your Typical Day? And

what about stuff like how the financial world works? How about How to Get into the Stock Market Without Losing Your Shirt, or even What That Information Sheet They Give You When You Open a Bank Account Means. I had to read *Lord of the Flies* in English class just to learn that all teenagers are animals at heart and thank you civilization for keeping us from ripping each other's throats out. But *Lord of the Flies* was written in 1954—haven't they written any good books since then? Maybe we would evolve if the curriculum did. How about a course called Marriage 101 or Mortgages 101 or Parenting 101? Some of the biggest things in your life and you don't get taught how to do them. But hey, I know the molecular difference between an acid and a base. I've got nothing against knowing the molecular difference between an acid and a base, but how about something practical once in a while? I just want to look around in the world and not be totally baffled by it, even as I recite the periodic table, you know?

So yeah, Bill, I've always had a problem with school.

All morning Hobbes followed me around in the hallways and in my classes, never in full view, always just behind me and to my right. Sometimes I caught a glimpse of the end of his tail. All morning I thought

the English project
the biology project
Hobbes
the English project

the biology project

Hobbes.

They were like mantras in my head.

They were like canker sores in my mouth.

They were like little rocks in my shoes.

I thought, I should go home. No, I can't go home. I should run away.

Hobbes: Hard to win the Change the World Lottery if you're a high school dropout.

Me: Or if you talk to imaginary tigers.

My parents didn't know that I was about to become the first ninety-sixth percentile to flunk. My dad had told me over and over again to do well in school so I wouldn't have to grow up to be a ditchdigger, and now that I was about to resign myself to a lifetime of ditchdigging, I realized I had never seen a ditchdigger anywhere ever and probably they had machines for that.

Hobbes: There's always McDonald's. I wonder if you worked there for, say, twenty years, you could afford to move out of your parents' house. I wonder if a guy whose great ambition is to be promoted from french fries to hamburgers could get a girlfriend.

On a day like this, of course, I couldn't get lucky enough to avoid Maurice.

Maurice: What do I have for lunch today, Timbit?

Hobbes growled.

Maurice grabbed my lunch bag and reached his huge hand into it. He threw the apple at me.

Maurice: You can have that.

He looked at me like he hated me for letting him get away with this every time he forgot his lunch, which was a lot.

Hobbes: Can I eat him?

Maurice: You're looking skinny, man. Tell your mom you need a bigger lunch.

He unwrapped my sandwich.

Hobbes: Not much to him.

Me: Eat him anyway.

Maurice leaned into me, slamming me against my locker.

Maurice: What was that?

Hobbes might have jumped him if Susie hadn't suddenly been standing there.

Susie: Everything okay, Calvin?

She glared at Maurice.

Hobbes: Babe!

Me: Your boyfriend is a bonehead bully.

I could say that because I knew Maurice wouldn't do a thing to me if Susie was there.

Susie: He's not my boyfriend.

Maurice: Bully? Strong word. I thought we were friends.

Maurice threw his arm around Susie's shoulders, grinned at me, and took a big bite of my sandwich.

She slid out from under his arm.

Maurice: Hey, where's your sense of humor, McLean? This is the way men show our affection. Right, Timbit? We're buddies, right?

Susie looked from me to Maurice and back again.

Me: Sure, Maurice. Buddies. Since first grade.

Maurice: Susie, you want half my sandwich?

She took it absently, and they walked away enjoying my peanut butter and banana sandwich. Susie looked back at me as if she was hoping I'd say something to Maurice, but I didn't. I never did.

Hobbes: I can't believe you're still putting up with that.

Me: Depends on what you mean by putting up with.

Hobbes: No wonder you brought me back.

Me: I didn't. I want you gone.

But at that moment I sort of didn't, Bill. I sort of liked him beside me in a corner of my mind, growling at Maurice and calling Susie babe.

The kids in the hallway were looking at me funny, possibly because it appeared I was arguing with myself, so I headed to English to eat my apple and wait for class to start. I don't know why I went to class—my life was over as far as school went. The project didn't have to be handed in until the end of class, and maybe I thought one would float down out of space and land on my desk.

All during class I was suffering the pains of the Damned Who Don't Do Their Semester Projects, and I thought I could hear the tiny screams of my brain cells as they died of grammar-review boredom. They started to get so loud I almost couldn't hear the teacher. She was looking at me, bending into that look, like she was seeing how repulsive I was for the first time, and suddenly she was revealed as the globular-faced alien she really was, and I understood that she was slowly turning the brains of young humans into a kind of gray smoothie and one day she'd stick straws up our noses and sip our brains out.

Teacher: Calvin?

I hadn't heard her question, but I sensed that under those buggy eyes was a subtle mind.

Me (politely): Could you rephrase the question, please?

She paused. Was she onto me?

Teacher: Where is the prepositional phrase in this sentence? I'm not sure how I could phrase it better.

Me: *In this sentence*. That's the prepositional phrase.

She stared at me. I thought I could see her jaw bubbling, as if her mandibles would break free of her human disguise any moment.

Teacher: Clever. But I was talking about the sentence on the board, not the one I was saying.

I looked at the sentence on the board. By now about a million of my brain cells had gone to their deaths, victims of grammar, but I tried to summon the survivors. I said something, but only nonsense came out.

Susie was looking at me like I'd sprouted a cancerous growth.

Susie: Calvin—?

All the colors in the room were a little too bright, the edges too black. Couldn't she see the evil intent of the so-called teacher? Hobbes was growling, low and deadly.

I stood up, but I felt wobbly.

Me: Run, Susie. I'll cover for you . . .

Teacher: Calvin? Calvin, are you all right?

But I wasn't, Bill. Something was wrong and Hobbes was roaring in my ears and the teacher had morphed into her true alien self and I could see Maurice laughing, and that's all I remember until I came to my senses in the hospital.

CALVIN'S ALTER EGO SPACEMAN SPIFF WAKES UP AND discovers that he has been abducted by aliens and is now restrained in a sterile laboratory in their ship. It is obviously an interrogation room, but Spiff is stoic and defiant. They have assumed the thin guise of humanoids, and this, Spiff decides, has been done to trick him into being docile as they perform their hideous experiments.

They poke needles into him and draw blood and ask him questions about the workings of his mind. At first Spiff refuses to give them what they want. He sees them conferring, deciding on the torture best suited to making him speak, and eventually they make him confess to everything.

Spiff despairs of his plan to save the world from a hostile takeover.

That's how it was, Bill. One minute I was this normal kid who uses his mind, and the next minute I was transmogrified into a kid whose mind uses *him*. I tried to figure it out, but how do you use your mind to figure something out if your mind is the problem?

I just kept thinking, me my name is Calvin, and why do I have a tiger purring in the corner of my room? I kept thinking this over and over until it occurred to me that it was possible something cosmic was happening here. Maybe Calvin was so real to so many people that on the day I was born, which was the day the last *Calvin and Hobbes* comic came out, maybe all that love and sadness people felt . . . I opened up my mouth to get my first breath, and I just sucked it in.

I wasn't sick. I was Calvin come to life!

Thinking about it like that, it was like all these pieces came together.

Of course, people probably wouldn't believe me. But hey, anytime something amazing happens in the universe we should pay attention, shouldn't we? When something is hard to believe, maybe it's the universe shaking things up a bit. Maybe it's saying, you haven't got me all figured out by a long shot. It's saying, I have a sense of humor, too.

I was lying there thinking about that, Bill, when my mom came in looking like she forgot to wear makeup and brush her hair. I knew she looked like crap because she was worried about me. Dad was right behind her, looking like he did at tax time, sort of tight and spooked.

Mom: Hi, Calvin.

Me: Hi, Mom. Hi, Dad.

Dad: Son.

Mom: I love you, Calvin.

Mom wasn't the gushy type, so I knew things were pretty bad when she said she loved me so early in the conversation and it wasn't even my birthday or anything.

Mom sat down on my bed. Dad didn't say anything, just kind of smiled, ruffled my hair.

Me: Dad, don't be sad. You were a good dad. Sometimes the polls were pretty low, but you weren't about the popular vote—you were about building character.

He bent down and put his forehead on top of my head.

Dad: My boy.

Me: Maybe if you weren't so strict. Maybe if you'd gotten me all the Christmas presents I asked for every year.

Dad: That must have been it.

Me: And TV—if you'd let me watch more TV.

Dad nodded.

Me: And making me take baths and go to bed at a reasonable hour and not letting me chew tobacco when I was six. I always thought it might push me over the edge. Oh, and don't forget you never built me that backyard ski lift. Ultimately everything is the parents' fault.

Dad: Everything.

He said it low and soft.

Me: But remember: just because your polls were low a lot

doesn't mean you don't have big fans. Doesn't mean some people don't love you so much.

A man came in wearing civilian clothes—jeans and a golf shirt.

Man: Hello, Calvin. I'm Dr. Filburn.

Me: Doctor, huh? Where's your degree?

Doctor: I have my diploma framed on the wall in my office. Would you like to see it?

Me: I hear those can be faked.

Dr. Filburn smiled. He was tall and had great muscles and looked like the kind of guy all the women in the world would probably want to date. He asked my parents if he could talk to me alone.

They went out and then the doctor asked me about what happened at school. Soon I was spilling the beans about Hobbes and my projects and Spaceman Spiff. I opened up about all that personal stuff, and he comes back with, you probably suffer from maladaptive daydreaming and the auditory hallucinations indicate you may have a more serious illness.

I decided to be polite.

Me: I'll take your thoughts under consideration, *Doctor*, but you should know that I wanted to go into neuroscience. I know brains. I might even have some.

Doctor: I'm sure you do. Let's invite your parents back in.

He asked them questions about their parents and siblings, and if I did drugs, and if they had noticed this or that or the other, and then he said he suspected that I may have had a schizophrenic episode but it would take observation over a period of time to confirm his diagnosis.

Mom listened to the doctor and nodded and tried to look like he'd just said I had a bad case of hangnail, and Dad looked like he wanted to punch him.

I kind of drifted off while he explained all about the brain to my parents and told them that schizophrenia was a family of psychiatric disorders, how it can be confused with other disorders, how symptoms range from slightly to totally disabling. Every time he said the word *schizophrenia* it felt like needles in my eyes, but then there was Hobbes sitting just out of my sight, yawning and licking his chops.

Dr. Filburn stopped talking and all three of them looked at me.

Me: Am I still going to grow up?

Doctor: I'm pretty sure you aren't terminal.

Me: Okay. So can I go home now?

Doctor: I'd like to keep you for a few days—to run some tests, come up with a plan for therapy and medication that will help you manage your symptoms and get you back to school. It's important to start treatment in young people as soon as possible. We'll change the course of treatment if the provisional diagnosis is wrong.

I thought it was time to reveal my new brilliant idea.

Me: This could all be cleared up pretty easily without medication. I just need Bill Watterson to make one more comic strip. Only one more comic strip, or even just one panel, of Calvin at age seventeen, healthy and well, with no Hobbes in it.

Doctor (staring):

Mom (staring):

Dad (staring):

Me: I've thought about it a lot, and I figured out that Bill Watterson and I have some universal connection. He made me this way and he could unmake me this way.

The doctor looked at my parents.

Doctor: This is one of the common symptoms of schizophrenia: delusions of inflated worth, power, knowledge, identity, or a special relationship with a famous person.

Me: Okay. But listen. I was born on the day, the very day, Mr. Watterson published his last comic strip and wrote a letter to the public saying he was done. Isn't that right, Mom?

Mom: Well, but we didn't know—

Me: And then! My parents named me Calvin!

Doctor:

Mom: Yes, honey, but you know we named you Calvin because your dad had just finished his PhD thesis on Calvinism. We'd never even heard of *Calvin and Hobbes*.

Me: Okay, but tell the doctor what Gramps did.

Mom: Well, he brought you a stuffed tiger—

Me: And put it in my bassinet right there in the hospital and said he wasn't going to have a grandson of his named after a man like John Calvin and by putting the tiger in my bassinet and calling the tiger Hobbes he renamed me even though my name was still Calvin.

Dad: This is all true, but—

He meant real.

Doctor: You have an interesting family. That does not mean Bill Watterson controls your destiny or can help you in any way.

Dad: Seriously, Calvin. You think you were made by Bill Watterson? I mean, I was there when your mother and I made you, and you don't want to make me tell you about it.

Me: I'm just like Calvin. You can't argue with that.

Mom: You're not like him. You—

Me: Have you read the strip?

Mom: Yes. Once. Your grandfather made me.

Me: So how am I different?

Mom: You have five fingers.

Me: Four fingers were symbolic.

Mom: Of what?

Me: Of how hard it is to draw hands. I have blond hair like him. I still have my red wagon.

Dad: Everyone's wagon is red.

Me (to Dad): You wear glasses.

Dad: So does your mom, unlike Calvin's mom.

Me: Maybe she wore contacts. I build the best snowmen on the block. And my first-grade teacher's name? Miss Wood! How close can you get to Miss Wormwood? Huh? Huh?

Mom: I admit, it's unusual, all those coincidences, but that's just what they are: coincidences.

Me: Is everything weird and unexplainable that happens in the world a coincidence? Are you sure?

Mom: Yes. I'm sure.

Doctor: Calvin, Bill Watterson has no ability to help you, and he doesn't have any wish to. Unlike me and your parents. We're going to do everything we can to get you well.

I didn't argue anymore. I didn't want Mom to be even sadder than she already was, watching her son Spaceman Spiff crash and burn as he entered the atmosphere of Planet Schizophrenia.

Doctor: I think Calvin needs some sleep. We'll talk again in the morning.

Mom: Yes, sleep sounds good.

Dad: We'll see you tomorrow, okay, Calvin?

Me: Okay. G'night.

My parents and the doctor left the room together, and Mom started crying before she was out the door.

Midnight, and I was still thinking about you, Bill, and me, and Hobbes, and Susie my ex-friend or frenemy or whatever she was. She was part of it, too. Half the night I thought about how I could convince you to do just one more comic strip, one starring seventeen-year-old me, alone without Hobbes. Just me, but without this illness. That's when I came up with my plan to prove my ultimate fandom so you would draw me that strip. I knew it would make me better. You could make me better, and make Hobbes go away.

Once I had my plan I could fall asleep, even though Hobbes was snoring.

THE NEXT MORNING DR. FILBURN CAME RIDICULOUSLY early.

Me: Sorry, but I don't display symptoms before breakfast.

I said that even though I could hear Hobbes taking a cat bath.

Doctor: Good to see you, Calvin. How was your night?

Me: Great. When can I get out of here?

Doctor: What's your rush? Aren't we treating you well?

Me: Can't you just, you know, open up my skull and adjust the dials a bit?

Doctor (smiles):

I decided to try reasoning with him.

Me: Grammar did it to me. Grammar and two big semester projects. I'm pretty sure if I could just eliminate grammar and homework from my life, I could just go home and be normal again.

Hobbes: Were you ever normal?

Me: This is all your fault, you flea-bitten, mangy furball—

Dr. Filburn studied me like I was a smear on a microscope slide.

Doctor: We're going to run some tests on Monday to see what's going on in that brain of yours.

Me: A tiger. A tiger is what's going on.

Doctor: I don't want you to worry. I'm sure we can help.

Me: Don't worry? I'm not worried. Why should I be worried? Just give me a choice between this and being boiled in oil and I'll go from there.

Doctor: Having a mental illness isn't a kind of death, Calvin. Not these days.

Me: Yes, it is. It's the death of normal. Maybe you haven't heard, but normal is what teenagers aspire to be above all else.

Doctor: Okay. So what's normal?

Me: Do you have a mental illness?

Doctor: No—

Me: That's normal. Normal is not sick. Normal is when you get to decide what's wrong with the other guy. Normal is blending in, like not having a psychotic episode in the middle of school, which makes you stand out.

Doctor: Calvin, do you know how many people in North America suffer from schizophrenia? I'll tell you. Over two million. You're not alone.

Me: Wow. If we were mutant zombie killers we could have taken over the world long ago.

Doctor: Many people with schizophrenia are very highly

educated and make significant contributions to society. You want to go to college? Get a good job?

I didn't say it, but suddenly I wanted it way more than I'd ever wanted anything before. I just wanted to be normal, ordinary, boring, and have a normal, ordinary, boring life.

Doctor: You can do pretty much what you want. Most people improve greatly on medications and lead productive lives. Nobody dies of schizophrenia.

Me: Unless they kill themselves.

Doctor (nodding): The risk of suicide is much higher. You're not planning to hurt yourself, are you?

I thought about my plan, but I was sane enough to know better than to tell him about it.

Me: No, but I do have a man-eating tiger here who is just waiting for me to weaken up. Which gives this whole thing a certain time sensitivity.

Hobbes growled and the doctor cleared his throat.

Doctor: Calvin, you are a very creative young man, which actually fits with some theories about people who experience hallucinations. Artistic people and highly creative people have a lower than expected density of dopamine receptors in the thalamus, as do people with schizophrenia. What that means is, your filter doesn't work as well as so-called normal people's. You've got this high flow of uncensored information coming in. In some people, that barrage of information makes them a genius in their field. We just have to get those negative effects under control, and then you can go have a great life—be the next John Nash or Salvador Dalí. We understand nowadays that it's not like you're either psychotic or not. Everyone is on a continuum.

Me: As in the space-time continuum?

Doctor: People can't be divided into happy people and depressed people. There are gradients. Some people only have the rare sad day, and some experience crippling depression. Most are a mix of both. Same with psychosis. I get a song stuck in my head, and you have a tiger stuck in your head. We're not fundamentally different. You stay with us here a few days, and we'll get you on a treatment plan that will alleviate your symptoms. Okay?

Me: I read antipsychotic drugs have side effects, like they shrink your brain.

Doctor: Every drug has potential side effects, Calvin. Patients may experience constipation, bed-wetting, drooling . . . decreased libido. But this is extremely rare.

Me: That's extremely not comforting.

Hobbes was laughing.

Doctor: These medications are a great advancement in the treatment of certain psychoses.

Me: No meds. Hobbes isn't that bad.

Hobbes: Not bad? I'm brilliant!

Me (to Hobbes): They want to medicate me.

Hobbes: That's because they think I'm an auditory hallucination.

Me: You are.

Hobbes: I am not.

Me: Are so.

Hobbes: Am not.

Me: Are so are so are so . . .

I realized the doctor was leaving the room, and I was talking out loud to nobody.

And that's why they want to put people on medication.

After I had breakfast I walked around the floor, which Dr. Filburn said I was allowed to do as long as I behaved myself. The people I saw didn't seem sick, or at least any sicker than what I saw in high school every day. The nurses looked a bit suspicious, like undercover spies or something. They pretended not to look at me when I checked out the doors, but I knew they were keeping their eyes on me. All the doors had coded access keypads, and a notice to visitors said the code was changed every few days and to check with the nursing staff.

In the common area I saw a woman who lifted her mug slowly to her mouth, her hand shaking, pinkie finger extended, bringing it almost to her lips, then slowly, carefully, as if she were placing the last card on a house of cards, set it back down on the table. She looked sad, as if she couldn't understand why she couldn't drink her tea. Then she did it again. The fifth time, I walked away.

A guy about my age saw me and saluted.

Soldier guy: Sir!

His hand was stiff in a salute over his right eye.

Me: At ease, soldier.

His hand dropped to his side.

Soldier guy: Got ourselves captured, sir.

Me: We sure did.

Soldier guy: I don't know how we can get away from them.

I was standing there looking at him, judging him, thinking this was my new peer group, when Hobbes spoke up.

Hobbes: You could slip out behind some visitors.

Me (to soldier guy): I don't know how to get away either, corporal, but I'm working on it. I'll let you know when I figure it out.

Soldier guy: Yes, sir. I'll await your orders, sir.

Hobbes: Tell him to drop and give you twenty.

I found a computer in the public reading room. I went online and checked out a map and the weather forecast. I'd saved eight hundred dollars in my entire life, which would pay for about eight days of college. Instead I would do this really cool thing with it. Next I sent a letter to the editor of your local paper, Bill, *The Plain Dealer* in Cleveland, telling him about the amazing plan I'd come up with. As you may know, I also sent an e-mail to you in care of your publisher, Andrews McMeel Universal. I felt better once the plan was in motion.

Then the place got pretty busy with visitors, and Hobbes and I went back to my room.

I WAS THINKING ABOUT MY GETAWAY WHEN I GLANCED up and saw Susie McLean standing in my room.

Hobbes: Hi, babe!

Susie McLean. The closest approximation to a friend that I've ever had. We've lived two doors away from each other since we were babies, and played together or fought together all growing up. She was just a part of my life—every neuron in my brain had a dendrite with Susie's name on it. And then a couple years ago she won the gene-pool lottery and turned out beautiful. Not long after that she started attracting a group of normal friends and hung out with me less and less. She hadn't really talked to me much in a whole year, so it didn't make sense that she'd be here now, standing in my hospital room.

She was wearing a T-shirt that said *Never trust an atom— they make up everything.*

She didn't say anything, just looked at me like she was surprised to see me lying there.

Me: Shouldn't you be in school?

Susie: It's Saturday.

Me: Why did you come here?

Susie: I was curious. Your mom told my mom.

Me: You wanted to see the schizophrenic kid?

She nodded. Not smiling. Not embarrassed. It's really hard to embarrass Susie.

Susie: Schizophrenia, hey?

Me: Well, they won't say for sure yet. The doctor says it will take a long time to confirm his diagnosis.

Susie: What does it feel like?

Me: Like my head is a transmogrifier gun—I have to be careful what I point my brain at.

Hobbes: It's a lethal weapon.

Me (to Hobbes): Careful or I'll aim it at you.

Susie: Who are you talking to?

Me: I was having a conversation with Hobbes, of which you only heard my part.

Susie: It's rude of you to have a conversation I can only hear one side of. Tell Hobbes that.

Hobbes: Babe, you are something. Tell Susie that.

Susie stared at me a bit more.

Susie: Maurice and his henchmen are making the most of your breakdown.

Me: Really? I'm surprised.

Susie: You are?

Me: No.

Susie: They're saying you're psycho.

Me: Kids these days.

Susie: Are you? Psycho?

Me: Can you hear Hobbes laughing at me?

Susie: No.

Me: Then yes, I am. You may not know that highly creative people who do well on tests of divergent thought have a lower density of dopamine receptors in the thalamus, as do people with schizophrenia. Schizophrenics and creative people have a lower degree of signal filtering, less sense of conventional limitations.

Susie:

Me: I'm creative. My thoughts diverge.

Susie: Hoo-boy, do they. When are you coming back to school?

Me: I'm not going back.

Susie:

Me: I can't go back. You know that. Teenagers have zero tolerance for people who don't come to consensus about reality.

Susie: You just don't want to go to school because you've never liked school.

Me: Yeah, but the weird thing is, my biggest fear now is that I won't be able to go back to school, or even to Earth. Everything I love is here on Earth.

Susie: I read online that some educated people and famous people and even rich people have schizophrenia.

Me: Don't say that word.

Susie: Is Hobbes still there?

Me: Yes.

Susie: Schizophrenia, schizophrenia, schizophrenia . . .

Me: Okay, okay!

Susie: I could bring your homework.

Me: I'm not doing my homework. I'm in a hospital. If I could do my homework, I wouldn't be in a hospital.

Susie: I'll help you.

Me: I'm sick. I'll do whatever I want. If you think I'm so weird you can always go, you know.

She started zipping up her parka.

Hobbes: You've always had a way with the girls.

Me: Wait. Susie, before you go, I have to tell you something. You're . . . you're part of it.

Susie: Part of what?

Me: Part of what's happening to me. Didn't you ever think about, you know, that you're named Susie, and you're friends with a guy named Calvin?

Susie: I always thought my parents didn't put much imagination into my name—

Me: I was born on the same day that Bill Watterson published his very last comic strip?

Susie: You've mentioned that.

Me: My gramps gave me a stuffed tiger called Hobbes? I'm hyperactive and pathologically imaginative? And then, even more amazing, a girl lives two doors down and her name is Susie!

Susie: I see. So my existence is merely an extension of your imaginary life.

I lay back on my pillows. I could hear Hobbes purring like a lawn mower.

Me: Maybe once you create an idea and millions of people are loving that idea, when you get brilliance and love all mixed up like that, it makes something that has to go somewhere. It impacts reality, like a meteorite hitting Earth. Bang! I think the universe just couldn't let Calvin go.

Susie: I'm sure they have a pill for that.

Me: I don't want to go on medication. I'm going to do something that will make me better, that will make Bill Watterson make me better.

Susie: Medication will make you better.

Me: I've asked Bill for one more comic strip, with Calvin, at age seventeen, in his right mind. No Hobbes.

Hobbes: Hey!

Me: I'm going to do something that will make him want to draw that comic for me.

Susie: So what is this thing you're going to do?

Me: What was the last thing Calvin said? He was outside in the snow, and he said, let's go exploring.

Susie: I remember.

Me: I'm going exploring. I'm going on a winter hike.

Susie: When? What about school?

Me: I told you, I can't go back.

Susie: So you're going to let Maurice and all the ignorant

people destroy your life? You're going to let them decide what you think of yourself and what you can do? Okay. Fine. Where are you hiking? Out of town?

Me: Out of the province.

Susie:

Me: Out of the country.

Susie:

Me: I'm going to walk to Cleveland, where Bill Watterson is reported to live.

Susie: Cleveland? From Leamington?

I nodded.

Susie (her voice becoming a bit intense): So you think that if you do this thing, Bill Watterson is going to make another Calvin comic when so far nobody else has managed to convince him? Not other famous comic artists, not his publishers, not his millions of fans? You think that you walking around Lake Erie is going to change his mind?

Me: Yeah, except for one thing. I'm not walking around the lake.

Susie: How are you going to walk to Cleveland if you don't walk around the lake?

Me: I'm walking *across* the lake.

Susie:

Me (grinning):

Susie (whispering): You think you're Jesus . . .

Me: On the ice! On the ice! How crazy do you think I am?

Susie: Crazy enough to be in a hospital ward for crazy

people. Did you know that every year people die on Lake Erie in the winter?

I was losing her. I could hear Hobbes laughing in some out-of-my-vision corner of the room.

Me: It's been below freezing for a month, and—

Susie: You're trying to kill yourself!

Me: Sooz, you have to do something big to get something big. Everyone wants more Calvin comics, but they don't need it. Not like me. And even if they did, they don't need it enough to do anything. Face it—nobody has tried very hard. This will be a pilgrimage, you know?

Susie: A pilgrimage to kill yourself. Besides, it's—it's manipulative.

Me: I'm not manipulating him. I'm just showing him how much I need him. People write letters to Bill, but nobody's done a pilgrimage.

Susie: And you think he'll be waiting on the other side? With this comic?

Me: That's the idea.

Susie stood staring at me, her eyes almost as big as her whole face.

Susie: Okay. Okay. Since your brain has lost all reason, let's remember at least that Bill's brain is not to be messed with.

Me: Maybe. But you never know about a brain like that. Bill is a genius.

Susie: He worked hard.

Me: What are the odds that you get both, genius and the ability to work hard?

Susie: One you're born with. The other you develop as you mature.

Me: There's always a trick, isn't there.

Susie: I'm going to tell your mom.

Me: If you do, she won't let me go.

Susie: Did you honestly think you could let me in on this and I wouldn't tell?

Me: They'll say I'm a danger to myself. They'll keep me in the hospital forever.

Susie: You are!

Me: You know I can do it.

Susie started shaking her head. Just a little shake, back and forth, while I talked.

Me: I was a Boy Scout, remember? You made fun of me?

She kept shaking her head like a bobblehead.

Me: I love to camp, even in the winter. You know that.

She stopped shaking her head.

Susie: You're really serious about this.

Me: I'm going to do it. You could make it hard for me, or easier.

Susie: What if you had a . . . a breakdown out there?

Me: I'm already broken. This is about putting the pieces back together.

Susie's hands were quiet at the ends of her arms. That was so cool about her. Other girls were always touching their hair or checking their nails or their phones or gesturing when they talked. Susie could be so still.

Susie: You didn't have to tell me.

Me: No.

Susie: You told me because you trusted me.

I shrugged, which meant, was I wrong?

She almost smiled, which meant, no.

Hobbes: You've never really understood women.

Me: Could you please just go away?

Hobbes: I want it to be like old times.

Me: It's not socially acceptable at my age to have an imaginary friend.

Hobbes: Do we care?

Me: I care! I hear you because I'm sick! I'm sick because I hear you!

Susie: I'm going to be kind and assume you're not talking to me.

Me: I'm leaving. Now. Before my parents show up.

Susie: I'm coming with you.

And that's when I realized she probably wasn't any more real than Hobbes.

I GOT DRESSED AND GRABBED MY PARKA AND WALKED
into the hall with Susie.

Me: Pretend you're just a visitor.

Susie: I am just a visitor.

Me: Pretend I'm just a visitor.

We sauntered behind two adults like they were our parents. Hobbes padded just behind me. I couldn't look right at
him no matter how fast I turned my head, but as we walked
toward the door I saw his front paw, which was twice as big
as my foot. I knew he wasn't there but mostly he was.

Nobody stopped us or even looked at us until the soldier
guy passed us in the hall. He saluted, and his arm fell.

Soldier guy: You're escaping.

Me: Yeah.

Soldier guy: You're going without me.

Me: I have to.

Soldier guy: Come back for me.

Me: I will.

I saluted him and he saluted me, and Susie and Hobbes

and I walked out of the ward doors behind some adults, just like that.

It occurred to me as we were walking that the soldier guy hadn't said anything to or about Susie. I stared at her, but her face didn't morph—okay, it was a bit woozy, but she was still pretty in a mean sort of way.

Me: Be gone, image.

Susie (sighing): I'm not an image.

Me: Images say things like that.

We found a cab waiting at the front doors of the hospital.

Susie: Where are we going?

Me: Campers Heaven.

She nodded.

It made no sense that this cute girl who had lots of friends and was good in school and who could probably have any guy she wanted was coming with me someplace. It also made no sense that Hobbes was in the backseat with us. I still couldn't see him, but somehow I knew he was there. I felt like you do in a dream where you realize you're dreaming and you think, well, as long as I'm dreaming . . .

We stopped at the bank on the way and then asked the cabdriver to wait outside while we were in Campers Heaven. The store smelled like tents and leather boots and granola, and I felt weirdly happy for the first time in what seemed like a long time.

Clerk: Hi, there. Can I help you with something today?

Me: Yes, I need to buy some winter hiking gear.

Susie: Two of everything.

Clerk: Certainly.

Me (to Susie): Hobbes doesn't need hiking gear. He has a fur coat, remember?

Susie: I'm going with you, remember?

Me: You said that just to bug me.

Susie: You want me to call your parents and tell them what you're doing?

Me: You wouldn't.

She folded her arms.

Me: Susie, this is going to be a seventeen-hour hike, maybe twenty. And you never know what conditions might be on the lake.

Susie: Two of everything. You knew I wouldn't let you go alone.

I stood there with my mouth open, and while my mouth was open all these thoughts blew in.

I remembered the exact moment when I realized I'd lost Susie. It was the beginning of eleventh grade, and we were standing at our lockers and she had just discovered the dead spider I'd put through her locker vent. She looked at it and she looked at me, but she didn't get mad. I couldn't figure out what she was thinking.

Did she feel sorry for me? And in the next second, she was swarmed by her girlfriends. They were all around her and you could see she had friends and I didn't.

Aside from Hobbes getting washed to death, that was probably my loneliest moment of all time. I guess if I had any excuse for letting things get as far as they did, Bill, it was because when she said she was going with me across the lake, I felt all that loneliness go away. It all sounds pretty lame now, but at the time . . .

Me: What's the first thing you pack on a winter hike?

Susie: Food? Toilet paper?

Me: Confidence. Believing you can do it.

Susie: And snow pants.

Me: Proper clothing is essential. But even more essential is staying clearheaded and calm.

Susie: Uh-oh.

Me (ignoring her): Synthetic fabrics, polypropylene is the best. If they get wet, they still insulate.

Susie: Oh, good. We'll be insulated all the way to the bottom of the lake.

Me: The lake is frozen up. Long underwear, synthetic or merino wool. Microfleece shirts, and we've already both got down parkas, hats, and mitts. We need good hiking boots, of course, waterproof and insulated, and big enough for two pairs of good socks. We need an extra pair of socks each, and probably another pair of mitts, and sunglasses.

It took a while to try on the boots, but otherwise everything went pretty quickly. We picked out food, water, a small tent, a flashlight, a compass, a tiny first-aid kit, and down sleeping bags. I could tell the clerk was impressed with my

vast knowledge. He just nodded and stacked everything beside the cash register.

Me: We still need backpacks, but they're pricey.

Susie: Maybe we should take a sled.

Somehow that felt like it had fate all over it, the idea of a
sled. It made the whole thing seem happier.

Me: Yeah, a sled! One of those, please, and a duffel bag
and a rope.

Hobbes: I'd like a scarf. A red one.

We bought the gear, excluding the red scarf, and put on
the clothes in the changing rooms.

Hobbes paced around the store, and I could hear him
sniffing hungrily at anything that looked like food. When I
tried to get a look at him from the changing room, he was
behind a rack of fleeces. When I came out of the changing
room, he was lurking behind a display of cast-iron pots. Soon
he was behind me again.

Hobbes: If you're a tiger, everything you need is already
attached to you. But a friend would have bought me a red
scarf.

When we left the store, I kept waiting for Susie to say just
kidding or to disappear. Instead she helped me load up the
trunk of the cab.

Me: You're not seriously coming.

Susie: You just bought me all this stuff.

Me: You can return it! Listen, you have to be the one who tells my mom that I'm at the bottom of the lake if I don't come home.

She got into the cab, and Hobbes and I got in, too, and I slammed the door.

Me: Point Pelee Park, please.

Cabdriver: Sorry?

Me: Point Pelee. Point Pelee.

Cabdriver: Okay.

He pulled away.

Me: Susie, please don't do this.

Susie: I won't if you won't.

She said it kind of sad, kind of scared, which made me feel sad and scared, which then made me mad.

Me: Look, I'm doing this. I didn't ask your opinion, and I don't want you to come. Why are you even here with me?

Susie: Because you need me.

Me: No, I don't.

Susie: I'm going to make sure you live and go back to school and become a neuroscientist and have a good life.

Me: Why are you talking like you care?

She appeared to consider this as if it were an honest question instead of a snide remark.

Me: You always thought I was weird. Last year you ditched me as a friend.

Susie: Yeah. You've always been weird. You're even weirder now.

Hobbes: You have to give her credit—she's always been smart.

Susie: You need to go back to school and face up to things. You need medication—

Me: Yeah—easy for you to say. You don't know what happens to a guy on some of those meds. Can I tell you?

Susie: No. We don't have that kind of relationship. Listen, if you go back to school, I promise I'll stand by you. So now can we just forget this whole impressing–Bill Watterson thing?

Me: Susie, I have to do this.

Susie: You really think Bill's going to be waiting onshore when you get to the other side of the lake?

Me: Yeah.

Susie:

Me: Well, maybe.

Susie: Don't be sad if he doesn't show up.

Me: I won't.

Susie:

Me: Okay, yes, I will.

Susie: I know.

We rode in silence the rest of the way. I sat close to Susie, crowded out by Hobbes. I kept looking at her, expecting she would vanish any second, but she was a persistent delusion if she was one.

Hobbes: I think she likes you. I can teach you how to smooch. I've had lots of practice.

Me: Move over.

Hobbes: Smooching is a way of tasting people without actually eating them up.

Me: Don't talk to me.

Cabdriver: Strange day to go to the lake.

Me: Yup.

Cabdriver: You sure are loaded up there.

Me: Yup.

Cabdriver: Pretty cold out there today.

Me: Sure is.

You could always tell when you were getting close to the lake. The lake opened up the sky. You could see the lake's sky before you saw the lake.

The driver was quiet for the rest of the way until we pulled into the park. We got out of the cab and the driver helped unload our stuff.

It cost $12.10 for park fees, and a flat rate of $40 for the cab.

Cabdriver: So, uh, you want me to come back for you later?

Me: Nope.

Cabdriver:

He looked from me to the sled to the lake and back to me.

Cabdriver: You're not—

Me: Yup.

The cabdriver stared at me a second.

Cabdriver: You're crazy if you're thinking of walking across that lake.

Me: Yes.

Cabdriver: Do your parents know?

Me: Hopefully this tip will buy your silence.

I held out the money and he snatched it.

Cabdriver: In my day kids killed themselves with heroin.

He jumped back into the cab and drove away fast.

Me: You meet all kinds when you're a cabdriver.

Hobbes: You should have tipped him more.

At first, Bill, I'd thought of heading south by southwest, passing Pelee Island along the way, maybe Kelleys Island, and ending up at Sandusky. We'd have Cedar Point to rely on if we ran into trouble. That was the shortest way, but I wasn't sure I should trouble you to drive all the way to Sandusky. That's why I decided to head south and south-east to end up at Cleveland in sight of the downtown towers, where you were supposed to meet us in two days in time for breakfast. That would be eighty-seven kilometers. The natural human walking gait is five kilometers an hour, which meant it could be walked in just over seventeen hours. Theoretically.

It sounded so feasible at the time, Bill. And you'd be there holding on to a new Calvin comic with no Hobbes in it that proved all the bad stuff that had happened to me was just for a laugh and tomorrow would be a whole new three-frame adventure.

That was the plan.

Too bad it didn't work out that way.

WHILE WE ATE LUNCH WE LOOKED OUT OVER THE LAKE.
The wind had blown the forming ice into sharp, angled ridges and chunks between the shore and the open ice.

The snow was white, the sky was white, the sun was white. Susie's face was white.

Me: It's 12:20. If we walk five kilometers an hour for the next six hours, we'll be in good shape to make it to the United States by breakfast the day after tomorrow.

Susie (in a small voice): Bill doesn't even know you're doing this.

Me: Yes, he does. I e-mailed him in care of his publisher, and they will have forwarded my letter to him. And I also sent a letter to the editor at *The Plain Dealer*. If the paper published it in their letters section or turned it into an article for the front page, Bill will read all about it.

Susie: Maybe he's drawing the comic right now so you won't have to do this.

Me: Bill didn't save Calvin from much. He let Hobbes tackle him every day after school.

Hobbes: He let him ride in his wagon with me on the back.

Me: He let him sled down that steep hill with Hobbes in the winter.

Hobbes: He let him jump out of his bedroom window on the second floor and let him get attacked by his food.

Me: He left Calvin alone with a tiger.

Susie: Yeah, I guess Bill isn't going to suddenly pop up and say, Hey, don't do it.

She turned to me.

Susie: He's not going to save you. *I'm* going to save you by telling you this is the craziest idea ever, and it just proves you're sick.

Me: It's a creative idea. I'm creative. The doctor says lots of creative geniuses have this problem. I read somewhere that John Lennon saw God in his living room.

Susie: Well, that was John Lennon, so it probably really was God.

Me: True.

I looked out at the lake again, and now I could see all the different colors of white in it. Blue-ice white, and lavender-white in the shadows of the drifts, and every kind of white ever invented. I looked at Susie and she looked back at me.

She couldn't be real. Nobody could be that pretty.

I looked up at the sky.

Me: Okay, universe, this is your chance to stop me. Send me a sign and I won't do it.

Universe:

I stood there and, Bill, I felt powerful somehow, like I was in control of me again. It was like the lake was invented for just this moment, and for me to walk across it. I packed our things in the duffel bag and roped it and the tent onto the sled.

Susie: I'm scared.

Me: It's beautiful.

Susie: It's empty.

I stepped onto the ice.

I didn't want her to come.

But I did.

I picked up the sled handle and looked back. Susie was staring down at her feet as if wondering why they weren't moving.

Me: Susie, meet me on the other side. How's that? Talk to Bill in case I'm a bit late.

Susie: You'll never make it without me. Do you know why you have to store your bottled water upside down?

Me: Why?

Susie: Because water in the bottle freezes from the top down. If it freezes up a bit, we'll still be able to drink some.

I didn't tell her I already knew that.

Susie: You need me.

I left it at that, Bill. I knew she would come. I guess I thought I could take care of her. That's how crazy I was.

I turned back to the lake.

Susie came to my left side, Hobbes to his spot just behind and to my right.

Me (to Susie): Okay. If we die, we die together.

Susie: You die first.

Hobbes: I'm already dead. Washed to death.

Me: Yukon ho!

We had begun.

The wind only whines and whistles and wails when it's trying to get into the cracks of windows and doors. It only thumps and bellows when it bumps up against trees and houses and cars. But on a big flat empty lake, it's just a force. It's a big soft hand that pushes and presses at you, silent, steady. Soon you realize the wind isn't flowing around you, over you, it's flowing through you, penetrating the electromagnetic field that gives you the illusion of being a solid entity, whipping straight through you, spinning your atoms like tops and leaving them dizzy and frosty and deeply impressed.

Me: Calvin likes snow.

Susie: Then you should be super-happy because I've never seen so much snow.

Me (pointing): All we have to do is head that way and we end up at Cleveland.

Susie: Bill Watterson would hate you to be doing this. He would call it a flare-up of weirdness. He would think you're trying to keep him from moving on in his life by wanting him to do another Calvin cartoon.

Me: I just want one. One comic, Calvin, aged seventeen, being of sound mind. Besides, what do you know about Bill Watterson?

Susie: As much as you!

Me: Nobody knows Calvin like I do.

Susie: How can you say that?

Me: Okay, when was Bill born?

Susie: July 5, 1958.

Me: Wha—? How—?

Susie: Is that the best you can do?

Me: What's his brother's name?

Susie: Thomas. Father, James. Mother, Kathryn. Wife, Melissa. Cat, Sprite, who has passed on.

Me: What did he almost call Calvin?

Susie: Marvin.

Me:

Susie (grinning):

Me: I told you all that stuff.

Even though I had no memory of telling her.

Susie: Yes, you did. And I remembered.

I couldn't believe the real Susie would remember all that about you, Bill. I didn't tell her I now had proof she was a delusion. I guess I thought a delusion was better than no-body at all.

We walked a long time, taking turns pulling the sled, keeping an eye on the compass. At least it felt like a long time, but when I checked my watch it had only been half an hour. I promised I wouldn't look at my watch again until an hour had passed.

White, white, flat, flat, white, white, flat, flat. My boots said it to me over and over. I felt like I was walking and not moving—the horizon the same, the snow the same, my boots sounded the same, white, white, flat, flat, white flat, white flat. Susie hiked with this glum look on her face, stomping like she was mad at the lake, like she wanted to get it over with as quickly as possible.

I checked my watch again. Twenty more minutes had passed.

Twenty?

My lungs were going into shock. They weren't used to such clean air. Where were the exhaust fumes, the spewings of factories and furnaces? the burning of fossil fuels? the crop-dusting, the insect killers, the fertilizer dust? This was Precambrian air.

I started to forget about my watch, about everything—noise and color and warmth and who I was and why I was there. Then Susie would sigh or say argh when we had to climb a snow dune, and I would remember that I was Calvin, the schizophrenic kid, the kid who was going to flunk twelfth grade because he didn't do his English and science projects, the kid who didn't tell his perfectly decent parents that he was going to walk across a lake and they would for sure know by now their son was missing from the hospital.

We talked to pass the time. Or at least I talked. About important stuff.

Me: What would it be like to be a bottom-dwelling fish?

Susie: Why do you ask questions like that?

Me: I mean, you would spend your whole existence in the cold and dark. Born in the cold and dark and always in the cold and dark, and when you died, it couldn't get any colder or darker than that, so you wouldn't even know that you had died—

Susie: Bonus.

Me: Did you know that you're probably the only one at school who wouldn't be freaked out by me, a person with schizophrenia?

Susie: That's not true. I am freaked out by you.

Me: I know why. I remind you that reality is just this game people play together, something their brain decides on, and the minute their brain gets iffy about reality, they realize everything they know about the world is just their own made-up version of it, and that would mean everyone is walking around in their own made-up world, all alone, and reality is just something we invent together to make us feel not so alone. It scares people when some of us check out of the game.

Susie: What makes you think you know what people think?

Me: Because brains are amazing. They can guess about each other. Think about it, Susie. The brain is the only part of your body that knows it exists. Huh? Huh? It knows! Your hand, it does what your brain tells it to. Your stomach, your lungs, your heart—your brain doesn't even ask your permission. It says, don't trouble yourself about breathing and digestion and blood and whatnot. Let me take caaaare of it for you . . . C'mon, what is scarier than that? The brain is a monster! Your feet don't know they exist. Your pancreas doesn't. They just do their good ol' job and die when the brain tells them to. But the brain, it says, try and figure me out, but you can only know as much as I'll tell you. Are you following me, Susie? The brain can ask bigger questions than you can answer.

Susie:

Me: Well?

Susie: I think I lost you back there somewhere.

Me: I see a town.

Susie: Of course there is no town out in the middle of the lake. You're hallucinating.

Me: You're right. Sorry.
Susie: There's a town in the middle of the lake!

Turns out it was an ice-fishing village, Bill. Just a bunch of little boxy shanties sitting on the ice—a few the size of big porta-potties, some as big as Dumpsters, a couple the size of sheds. One was painted up to look like a doghouse. One was painted with palm trees and flowers and a hula dancer. The village came complete with a chapel shanty and a theater shanty, and between all the shanties were little roads made of snowmobile tracks.

It was cool, like the lake had surprises.

A man came out of one shanty and stopped to look at us. He was carrying a fishing pole. He was six and a half feet, probably close to three hundred pounds.

Hobbes: I'm hungry.

Me: Catching anything?

Fisherman (suspicious): Just a cold.

Me: Interesting place.

Fisherman: 'Tis. Quiet. Nobody minds your business. Fishin'?

Me: No.

Fisherman: Whatcha doin' out here if it isn't fishin'?

Me: We're hiking across.

Fisherman: You're hiking across the lake? You're nuts.

Me: That's the point.

Fisherman (stroking his beard): What are your names?

Me: Calvin and Susie.

Hobbes: And Hobbes.

The fisherman stopped stroking his beard.

Fisherman: Calvin and Susie, huh.

He said our names like he didn't believe us.

Fisherman: No way should you be doing this.

Me: I have to.

Susie: He has to.

Me: She doesn't have to. Can you give her a ride back to shore?

Susie: He doesn't tell me what to do.

Fisherman: Okay, I'm sorry, but I'm going to have to contact the authorities.

Me: Cell phones don't work out here.

Fisherman: I have a ham radio.

Me: Please. We're on a trek to prove our devotion to the creator—

Fisherman: Creator? Are you some kind of religious nut?

Me: The creator of *Calvin and Hobbes*.

Fisherman:

Me: Well, we'll be going now.

Fisherman: You're doing this for . . . for Bill Watterson?

Me: Yes.

Susie: We're doing this to raise awareness for schizophrenia.

Me: We're doing this to show how much we want Mr. Watterson to draw one more Calvin comic. He might even be waiting for us on the other side of the lake.

Fisherman: I love him. I have every book.

Me: Yeah. Me, too.

Fisherman: When Watterson stopped, I felt like somebody I loved died. I mean, I cried.

Me: I understand.

Fisherman: You're serious about this.

Me (nodding):

Fisherman: Okay. I'm going to give you the shortest lesson on ice I can. You listen up. It's probably safe, given that we've had a month below freezing. But if you see logs, stumps, rocks, anything sticking up out of the ice, you stay away. They pick up heat from the sun in the day and make weak moats of ice around them. If the ice looks gray and pebbly, that's rotten ice. It forms in a snowstorm and all those trapped air bubbles are bad news. Another thing—you see water on top of ice, you beware. Water is heavier than ice and it creates fractures called honeycombs. Honeycomb ice is deadly. Discolored snow might mean slush: avoid. If the snow is even and you see a sudden depression? Avoid. If you see a straight open crack, not to worry—they can freeze over. But if two or more cracks meet, avoid. You got all that?

Me: Yes, sir.

Susie: Got it. Logs, gray and pebbly ice, water on ice, discolored snow, depressions, and more than one crack.

69

Fisherman: This lake, she's a bit o' ocean, left over from a dinosaur ocean, and she has suffered. She has had to swallow boats. There's a Civil War tugboat down there, preserved in the cold water. In 1841 the steamship *Erie* burned, killin' 250 people, and they say you can still see it burnin' sometimes out on the water. In 1923 Chevy made a coupe with engines that used copper cooling fins and suffice to say they were a fire hazard. So GM recalled them all— 498 of them—and dumped them in Lake Erie. And then the people on the bottom, of course. She doesn't like it. The lake, she looks pretty, but people forget she's a force to be reckoned with. She's a sea, and she doesn't like any human garbage. You remember that. Don't make her suffer any more than she already has.

Me (nodding):

Susie (nodding):

Fisherman: Lake Erie has her monsters, too. Jenny Greenteeth, she's a monster that can see up through the ice. Then there's the Black Dog of Lake Erie. He appears on ships before they go down to the bottom. And of course there's South Bay Bessie, the sea monster.

I'd heard of South Bay Bessie, the forty-foot serpent that was sighted every so often in Lake Erie. Even the Seneca Indians knew about her.

Fisherman: So now I've told you about the lake, do you really mean to do this thing?

Susie:

Me: Yes.

He opened our duffel bag and dug around in our gear.

Fisherman: Seems like you got what you need.

He rubbed his beard a moment, considering us, and then he shoved his hands in his coat pockets.

Fisherman: Tell him about me. Bill Watterson, I mean. When you see him, tell him about me.

Me: I will.

Fisherman: Tell him my name. Orvil Watts.

Me: Orvil Watts.

Orvil: Wait . . . !

He slipped back into his shanty and came out with a bag.

Orvil: Cookies.

Hobbes: Cookies!

Orvil Watts put the cookies in the duffel bag.

Me: Thank you. You're not going to make that call, though, right?

Orvil: No. I get it now. Walk on.

Susie and I walked on, pulling the sled. I looked back once, but Orvil was gone.

Trudge, trudge.

That was the language of boots.

They only said one thing now—trudge, trudge—but it

was possible that boots had a sophisticated poetry that only they could hear with their rubber ears and speak with their rubber tongues.

Susie: Well, this is exciting.

Trudge, trudge.

Susie: Yes, everybody's going to be über-impressed with this.

Trudge, trudge.

Susie: Yup, here we are, out on the bald, boring, frozen lake . . .

Me: It doesn't have to be exciting. It just has to be a pilgrimage. That's all Bill cares about.

She stopped.

She was still a moment. She bent down and picked up a wad of snow and threw it at me.

Thwap.

Right in the face.

She always was a good shot.

Hobbes laughed.

I started making a snowball and she ran away.

Me (running after her): Bill will understand. I'm Calvin, remember? I was always doing stuff he didn't like or agree with.

Hobbes: The embodiment of human stupidity.

Susie turned back toward me. I chucked the snowball, but it didn't connect.

Susie: Calvin, just think about it. If Bill pays the slightest attention to this, just imagine the crazies that would come out!

We looked at each other and laughed until we had to sit down.

Susie's face changed when she was laughing. It went all soft and relaxed, and stayed that way for a while after she stopped.

Susie: I haven't laughed like that in—

Me: In a year?

She frowned and stood up.

Susie: We'd better get going.

WE WEREN'T MAKING NEAR THE TIME I'D THOUGHT. It was slower going when you were walking on snow and around chunks and ridges of ice. But it felt good to be in the dimension of nothing. Close to four o'clock now, the sun was lower on the horizon, a whiter hole in a white sky. It didn't shine. It looked like a dead sun, a ghost sun, as if the heat had all burned out of it. You could look right at it. We had maybe two hours before dark, so we had to make good time.

I couldn't hear anything but my own breath and my boots and Susie's boots like an echo after mine. The sled felt like it was loaded up with lead. I could hear Hobbes snoring, so I figured he was taking a ride.

Spaceman Spiff had been disconnected from the spaceship and was just drifting, drifting, drifting away into the vacuum. Earth kept getting smaller until it was a blue basketball and then a blue baseball and then a blue marble, and he stared and stared until it was a blue dot. His air ran out and his body died, but weirdly he didn't decay in the vacuum of space, and one day an alien garbage man picked him up and Spiff's eyeballs were wide open and filled with shiny blue atoms—

Susie stopped. For a second I'd forgotten how to stop, and then I remembered.

Susie: Listen.

She was staring into the sky, staring like a blind person would stare—unseeing, listening with her whole body.

Me: What?

Susie: What do you hear?

Me: My breathing.

Susie: No, Calvin. Listen. Just listen.

So I listened.

When you've lived all your life with the sound of Life in General, you don't even hear it anymore. You don't hear the noise of cars, trucks, trains, airplanes, refrigerators, air conditioners, furnaces, and you don't feel radio and television waves shooting through you, and you don't hear telephones, animals, birds, floors creaking, doors opening, the voices of six billion people all talking and laughing and crying, and over a billion cows mooing and nineteen billion chickens clucking and a million species of bugs buzzing, and you don't realize that it all adds up to this low hum of Life in General.

Life in General doesn't live in the middle of the lake.

Me: It's quiet.

Susie had closed her eyes. She didn't answer me.

My ears started straining for something, like they had this need to hear something, anything, like that little eardrum needed something to beat its bongos. After a long moment, I did.

Me: It's the sound a planet makes when it travels a hundred thousand kilometers an hour through space.

Susie: It's a truck.

Me: Huh?

Susie: That sounds like a truck!

Hobbes: A planet spinning through space sounds like a truck?

Susie (turning): Calvin—

We turned around.

A truck was coming.

A gray truck.

Coming straight at us.

Me: It's a truck.

Susie:

Me: On the lake—driving on the lake—

Susie:

Me: Tell me you see that.

Susie: I see it.

The truck slowed down as it pulled up beside us. It had no doors or roof, but it was a truck.

A man wearing a plaid hat with earflaps nodded to us, as if he met people walking on the lake all the time.

Plaid-hat guy: Have you seen Fred?

Me:

Susie: We . . . we don't know a Fred.

Plaid-hat guy: Okay. Thanks.

Me: Bit chilly without the doors and roof of your truck?

Plaid-hat guy: We take 'em off. If the ice breaks, we can jump out.

Me: Oh.

Susie stared down at the ice.

Plaid-hat guy pulled away.

Me: Okay, a truck just drove up to us on the ice and asked for Fred. Sometimes the world is crazier than me.

Susie (staring after the truck): Stuff like that only happens when I'm with you.

She looked doubtfully at the ice and started walking.

YOU KNOW HOW IF YOU STARE AT CLOUDS LONG ENOUGH you start to see shapes? The same thing happens with snow. You don't just see snow anymore. It has textures and colors and shapes: snow like silk, like a wedding dress; snow like slabs of cement, like the lake was an abandoned construction site for ice palaces; snow like crunchy cookie crumbs; snow stretched and blown and fine as desert dunes. And maybe, Bill, the same thing happens with people if you spend enough time with them or think about them enough.

That's what was happening to me, walking beside Susie hour after hour. Here on the lake she was tough and gutsy. Growing up with her I just took her for granted. She was just this kid who was always there when I wanted to hang out with someone or bug someone. And now she was like this woman, this strong woman who was doing this thing with me.

Susie: How far do you think we've gone?

I knew we weren't doing five K an hour, and I was worried we weren't even doing four.

Me: I'm sure there will be a sign soon to let us know how far we've come.

Susie: Clever.

Me: My brain I offer to the gods.

Susie: What makes you think they want it?

Me: What makes you think I want it?

Calvin the human furnace moves forward on his mission to cross the arctic lake. The human furnace and his companion are tiny hot spots in a wasteland of frozen cold. Together they trudge, partners in their dark destiny, willing to share in the glory of success or the ignominious fate of defeat.

Me: Trudge, trudge.

Me: Trudge, trudge.

Me: Trudge, trudge.

Susie: You're driving me crazy.

Me: Welcome to my world.

Susie: I know we're trudging, I don't need the voice-over.

We trudged and I didn't say the word *trudge* once. Susie took over the compass because I kept forgetting to look at it.

Hobbes: I know why you did this. You did it on purpose knowing that I'm a jungle animal and I don't like the cold. You want me to freeze to death.

Me: That would be a bonus.

Hobbes: Why do you want to get rid of me? I'm your friend.

Me: Are you sure you're my friend?

Hobbes: I've never eaten you. Doesn't that prove my undying friendship? I'm here to protect you, and to make sure you don't give up on winning the Change the World Lottery.

Me: You're not protecting me. You're the thing I need protecting against.

Hobbes: I could help you with Susie. I've got a way with the babes.

Me: We're on a hike, not a date.

Susie: You got that right. Other guys take me to the movies.

Me: Let's remember I didn't ask you on this date.

Susie: That was very gallant of you to say.

Me: But I'm glad you came.

She stopped.

Susie: You are? You admit it?

Me: It's easy to admit things to a figment of your imagination.

She laughed.

That was a bad sign. The real Susie would have punched me in the arm.

Susie (frowning, looking down): Calvin, I'm sorry.

Me: You should be. What are you sorry for?

Susie: For ditching you to hang out with other people.

Me: Oh that.

Susie: Turns out they were boring.

Me: Even the guys you dated?

Susie: Especially them.

Me: And I'm not? Boring?

Susie: No. Sometimes I wish you were a bit more boring.

Hobbes: You are boring. You keep telling me to go away. When did you get so boring?

Me (to Hobbes): I can't play my life away. There's this thing called growing up. It's essential for functioning in the adult world.

Hobbes: The adult world is highly overrated.

Me: It's the only one I know of for people over a certain age.

Hobbes: We could have our own world.

Me: Bill Watterson is in the adult world and I—

Hobbes: Bill Shmill. Also highly overrated. Why do you keep talking about him like he's the creator of the known universe?

Me: Hey! You wouldn't exist without him.

Hobbes: Remember what it feels like to wake up on a summer morning and not think about anything except going outside and sitting under a tree? You've forgotten. I bet Bill has, too. Instead of a heart you'll have an iPhone. Instead of a brain you'll have pings that tell you what has to be done that day and that minute. You'll never sit in a tree house again, or build a snow fort. You'll rake and shovel walks, instead. But it doesn't have to be that way, ol' buddy . . .

Me: Susie—

Susie: Oh, you're talking to me now? Please, don't let me interrupt what must be a scintillating conversation—

Me: Do you know what the default network in your brain is?

Susie: Yes, I know what the default network is.

Me: You do?

Susie: Of course I don't! I'm normal! Normal people don't know all this stuff about their brains.

Me: So the default network consists of three main regions: the medial prefrontal cortex, the posterior cingulate cortex, and the parietal cortex.

Susie: Sounds like a fabric for fitness wear.

Me: All these parts of our brain talk to each other, like social networking. The medial prefrontal helps us imagine ourselves as individuals and also the thoughts and feelings of others. Animals have trouble with that—this is a thing that makes us human.

Hobbes: Hey!

Susie: Can you imagine my thoughts and feelings right now?

Me (ignoring her): All those brain bits give you this sense of yourself, like you're the star in the movie of your life. But people who have schizophrenia, their medial prefrontals go on strike—malfunction, malfunction. We're thinking, all right, but we don't know where the thoughts are coming from, so it feels like someone is putting thoughts in our heads, or someone is reading our minds.

Susie: You are so weird.

She stopped suddenly and sat on the sled.

Susie: I have to sit.

I sat beside her. I reached into the duffel bag and pulled out two granola bars. We peeled the wrappers off and ate slowly. I threw a piece behind me for Hobbes.

Susie: What are you doing?

Me: Feeding Hobbes.

Susie: That's a waste of food.

Hobbes: That's a matter of opinion.

Susie was staring out over the lake.

Me: You okay?

Susie: It's beautiful, really, isn't it.

Me (stomping the ice): What, this old thing?

She didn't smile.

Susie: This emptiness. I bet we're the only ones who have come this far. It's been this beautiful and strange on the lake every winter forever, and nobody knew about it and nobody cared and it still went on being beautiful. Just because.

Sometimes Susie was hard to figure out, but she just went on being beautiful and strange forever. I had watched her around the kids at school, and she was never like this with them, never raw like she'd bleed if you touched her.

Susie: Doesn't it make you feel kind of awesome that the

world is beautiful for no other apparent reason than that it is? Like beauty has its own secret reason. It doesn't need human eyes to notice. It just wants to be glorious and unbelievable.

Me: You're unbelievable.

Susie had been breaking off bits of her granola bar and eating them as if her hands were part of her digestive system before teeth. After a minute she looked at me.

Susie: You're not following that up with a sarcastic comment?

Me: No.

Susie: That was a major step forward in our relationship.

I didn't answer because the word *relationship* was pinging around in my skull.

Susie: Do you ever wonder what life is all about, Calvin? Yeah, I know you do. You're one of the few guys I personally know who stop to wonder about that. For me—I don't know what it's all about, but I've decided maybe that's the cool thing about it. Life lets you decide for yourself. I mean, it would be awful if it wasn't up to us, wouldn't it? If life said, this is what I'm about and don't go getting any ideas of your own?

Me: So have you had any ideas?

She nodded.

Susie: As weird as it sounds, I got an idea a long time ago that you were one of the things my life was about.

Me: When you say you, do you mean me?

Susie (ignoring me): I didn't know what that would mean. Maybe it would be just something I felt and wouldn't add up to anything. Maybe I'd just, you know, keep newspaper articles about you in an album if you became famous. Or maybe if you became a starving artist I'd have to send you money in unmarked envelopes. But then you got sick and I thought maybe it meant that I was supposed to be there for you, or— or help in some way.

We were quiet for a while.

Me: You're wrong about us being the only ones who have ever seen this. Walter Lick walked across the lake in the winter of 1912, Gene Heuser in 1963, and Dave Voelker in 1978. Who knows if there's been anyone since.

Susie: Did they live?

Me: Barely.

Susie: Barely is better than nothing.

We finished our granola bars and got walking.

I felt like I could walk to the moon, Bill. I was on this hike with a girl who could see something beautiful on a vast, empty, eerie, frozen lake. Underneath the ice it was dark and cold and mysterious, but all she saw was the beauty and awesomeness of it.

I actually almost forgot about Hobbes for a while, and then he was there again.

Hobbes: Thanks.

Me: For what?

Hobbes: For nothing.

Me: What?

Hobbes: How come I only get one bite of granola bar? Don't let me get too hungry.

IT WAS GETTING DARKER, AND I WAS ABOUT TO SUGGEST
we set up the tent, when we came to the cars.

I dropped the sled handle.

Me: I'm hallucinating again. Still.

Susie: It's catching.

Me: What are you seeing?

Susie: Cars . . . nine of them. And a truck.

Me: A car lot in the middle of Nowhere, Lake Erie.

Susie: That's what I see.

Me: Do you see any people?

She shook her head.

Me: Me neither.

We both stared, and the cars stared back.

Susie walked right up to an old GMC, pulled on the door
handle, and it opened easily.

She grinned.

I went around to the other side and slid in shotgun.

Susie: This one is mine. Go find your own.

I checked out a couple of rusted and banged-up cars

before I saw a really beat-up old Mustang with the backseat ripped out. I whistled and slipped into the driver's seat.

After a bit Susie got into the Mustang beside me.

Me: Hey, I thought you had your own.

Susie: I'm just visiting.

I gripped the steering wheel and stared out the windshield, grinning my face off. Susie grinned back.

Me: Sooz, do you believe in God?

Susie: It's easier when he just gave us free cars.

Me: Yeah, and even easier when he gives you keys!

Susie: What?

I turned the ignition. It whined for a long time and then it came to life.

I tore away and she screamed and laughed and I pressed the gas pedal to the floor and we zoomed away over the ice and fishtailed and made donuts and came back and zoomed around a few minutes more until it ran out of what must have been the tablespoon of gas that was left in it.

Susie: This lake is freaky.

Me: Yeah. But in a good way, right?

She grinned.

Me: Vroom, vroom . . . vrooooommmm!

Susie: (gasp)

Me: What?

Susie (whispering): I know why they left the cars. They're dumping them!

Me: Well, they're not selling them, that's for sure.

Susie: Calvin—remember what Orvil said? About how they treat the lake? I bet people drive cars out here where nobody will see and leave them on the ice so they'll sink to the bottom of the lake when spring comes. Maybe they know where the weak spots on the ice are, or where the ice breaks up early. Come on!

We got out of the Mustang. We had to walk a ways north to get our sled, and then we started heading south across the lake again.

Hobbes: What a waste.

Me: They could have donated them.

Susie: To the poor.

Me: To poor teenagers.

She looked around at the empty white lake.

Susie: How can they do that to our lake?

Me: It's our lake now, is it?

Susie: It's ours because we know it this way.

Me: Bill wouldn't have been impressed if we'd driven across the lake.

Susie: He won't be impressed that you're walking across it either.

She stopped and looked back. It was dark enough now that the cars seemed ghostly from where we were.

Susie: We made that up.

Me: If we did, it was a good one.

———

I didn't want to put the tent too close to the cars, so we walked a little farther.

We'd just rounded another snow dune when we saw a light up ahead, floating in the dusk like a square moon.

Me: Is that real?

Susie: As real as my right arm.

This did not reassure me.

It was an island, a really small island.

With a little cabin on it.

Smoke drifted out of the pipe chimney. A fire was going in that cabin.

I thought we would reach it in a couple of minutes, but it was farther than it seemed. We got out our flashlight and twenty minutes later we scrambled up the rocks on the shore of the island, dragging the sled behind us.

A huge man opened the door. His beard covered almost all of his face except his lips, his upper cheeks and eyes, and his forehead. Those were covered by bushy eyebrows and a mane of curly gray head hair. He looked like a big gray bear with human eyes.

Hobbes: Yeti?

Man: I thought I was seeing things.

Me: I know the feeling.

Man: I thought I must be seeing things because no way would two kids be out for a stroll this far into the lake, and at night.

He sounded angry. He took a step toward us, onto the wooden box that served as a front stoop. Susie and I backed up.

Man: I thought, they got a sled. They turned right when they should've turned left, those two. They want a hill, not a lake, those two. You know the difference between a hill and a lake, boy?

Me: We—

Man (his voice getting louder): Then I see one of you is a boy and one of you is a girl, and no way should a girl be in the middle of this lake.

Susie scowled at him.

Man: So I'm thinking that the boy should be the one held responsible for the girl being out in the middle of the big, very big lake.

Susie and I glanced at each other and started to leave.

Man: Git in here!

Me: Thanks, but no, sir. We have to be getting on our way, sir.

Man: You stay out then. Come on, girl, I've got a fire, and I'm not near as scary as I seem. Come on, this house isn't made of candy and I'm not going to stuff you into the oven.

She pointed at me.

Susie: I'm with him.

Man: All right then. Both of you, in. Grab a bit of fire. Name's Noah.

Me: I'm Calvin, this is Susie.

I said it cheerfully in my best un-schizophrenic voice.

Susie: Calvin didn't tell me about any islands out here.

Noah: It's a reef. Not on the map.

We walked slowly through the door of the cabin. Noah gestured to two chairs at a small wooden table.

Noah: Throw your coats there.

Hobbes: Will there be hot chocolate and marshmallows?

The fire was a beautiful thing. I was almost willing to be thrown into it, if that's what he meant to do to me.

In the cabin was

a narrow bed heaped with quilts

a coatrack with various ratty coats on it

a duffel bag, open, full of books

some shelving with cans of food on it

a small round table stacked with papers and pencils

two old wooden chairs

a stool hanging from the rafters

various bins

and a door to another room—probably the privy.

We took off our parkas and mitts and boots and socks and held our sore feet to the fire.

Hobbes stretched out close to the stove, still just out of my line of vision.

Noah: Figure you two have a reason.

Susie: We're hiking across the lake.

She pointed at the door to the privy.

Susie: May I?

Noah: It's basic.

The minute she shut the door he looked hard at me.

Noah: Walking across the lake is something only seasoned hikers would do, boy, and only after they studied maps and depth charts and weather reports. And even then they wouldn't do it.

Me: I know how far it is south to the Ohio shore. And I know the lake is the shallowest of the Great Lakes, but still plenty deep enough to drown in. And I know it's cold outside.

Noah (not looking at me, speaking to the fire): Worse than an idiot to bring a girl out here.

Me: I know.

Noah stood up, opened a door in the back, and returned with a big chunk of wood and a loaf of bread. He threw the wood into the belly of the woodstove and put the bread to warm on top.

Noah: You got a story. Why you wanna do the lake? And you'd better talk to me or I'll be notifying the coast guard, you can bet on that.

Me: I'm on a pilgrimage.

Noah: And you didn't want to go alone.

Me: She . . . she wanted to . . .

He looked at me like I was a big, disgusting insect.

Susie came out and sat next to me.

Noah glowered at me.

Me: So you live here, Noah? Year-round?

He ignored me.

Susie: Do you?

Noah: I come here off-season. Do a little ice fishing. Do a little poetry.

Me: Poetry?

Noah (to the air): I'm talking to the little lady.

He didn't look like a poet. Not that I'd ever seen one before.

Susie: No one at home to care that you're out here all alone?

Noah: My wife cares. Cared. She's divorcing me.

Susie: I'm sorry.

Noah drew his arm across his nose, and I realized he'd started to cry. His facial hair was soaking his tears up like a sponge.

Noah: She said she'd take me back if I figured it out.

Susie: Figured what out?

Noah: She said I'd have so much time out here alone, she was sure I'd figure it out. It's like she gave me a puzzle to solve, but I just sit here and think about it for hours and never figure it out.

Susie shook her head sadly.

Noah: The only clue she gave me was that I spent all my time digging around inside myself for poems, but I didn't think about the inside of her. She said, stop stuffing metaphors between you and me. What does that mean?

He opened a huge can of beans and dumped them into the dirty frying pan on the stove beside the bread and put a kettle on, too.

Noah: She's my muse, you see. If I lose her, I lose what makes the poems in me.

Susie: Maybe she wants you to be with her, instead of here.

He shrugged.

Noah: Can't live among the civilized all year. Can't bring a woman out here.

He glared at me, his eyebrows almost covering his eyes.

Noah: Unlike some people. And you, little lady? What's your story?

So Susie explained everything to him, about how we'd known each other all our lives and how I talked to an invisible tiger and got diagnosed with schizophrenia, and I had decided that if Bill Watterson would draw another cartoon with Calvin okay in it, and no Hobbes, I would be okay, too, and how I knew I had to walk to Bill like a pilgrimage, but not an ordinary walk, it had to be big, and I came up with this stupid idea, and how she wouldn't let me go without her because I didn't have a clue.

She talked about me like I wasn't sitting right there, and he listened like I wasn't sitting right there.

When she stopped, he was silent for a minute. Then he scooped most of the beans into a big bowl and gave us two spoons. He tore a hunk of bread off for himself and gave us the rest. I was so hungry I dived in. He ate his beans out of the pan.

I'd never tasted anything as good as those beans and bread, ever.

Me: Thank you.

He ignored me.

Susie: Yes, thank you.

Noah: You're welcome.

We ate in silence for a while—silence except for the fire falling and popping, and the wind outside. Noah was looking at the beans as if they held the meaning of life in their little beany hearts. He put the pan back on the stove.

Hobbes: If I can't eat him, can I have those beans?

Me: No. Have some of my bread.

I threw a piece behind me and looked up to see Noah and Susie staring at me.

Noah (to Susie): Schizophrenia, huh? You ever heard of Max Planck?

Susie (shaking her head, her mouth full):

Me: Uh—he's the quantum theory guy, right?

Noah: Ol' Max, he said there is no matter the way we think of it, that all matter is just a whole universe of atomic particles vibrating together in a way that makes it look like stuff and feel like stuff.

Susie and I kept eating the beans and bread like it was the food of the gods.

Noah: So other people, they take this fact and figure out that the world vibrates at seven hertz. The world and everything in it, cats and balls and books and spoons and hammers and mountains and all of it, including the human brain: seven hertz. It's a seven-hertz world. So here's all the world vibrating along at seven hertz in harmony with the universe, and then along comes a ten-hertz person.

Me: Ten hertz?

Noah:

Susie: Ten hertz?

Noah: Yup. Ten hertz. That's what the schizophrenic brain vibrates at. Ten hertz. That's what some say anyway. Some say you're accessing other times or places or dimensions or worlds, you're seeing things in the dimension of ten hertz and it's just as real as the seven-hertz world.

He picked up his beans again, and Susie and I stared at him like he'd just started speaking in ten-hertz language.

This guy was smart. This guy got me!

Suddenly I wished he could stand me.

He looked at Susie.

Noah: Of course that doesn't mean you can let his reality boss yours.

Susie: Whenever his and mine disagree, he gives in to mine. That's the rule with us.

Hobbes: Do you think a tiger in our reality could eat a poet in his reality?

Me: In my reality we are dropping the subject, Hobbes.

Noah (to Susie): Is he for real talking to Hobbes again?

She nodded.

The fire in the woodstove snapped and roared. Noah's talk made me remember an interview you'd given once, Bill. You said Hobbes wasn't a doll that magically came to life when Calvin was around. You didn't think of him as Calvin's imaginary friend either. You said Calvin had his version of reality and everyone else had theirs, and they both made sense.

Calvin thinks, therefore he is. In his conscious experience lies the theory of everything—new dimensions surround him like falling tinsel, like bubbles falling, down and down, breaking on him . . .

Noah (putting down his pan): So. Bill Watterson. Met him once.

SUSIE AND I BOTH LOOKED UP SHARP, BUT HE WAS
poking at his fire.

Me: Nah. You didn't.

Noah:

Susie: Really?

Noah: Nice guy. Quiet-spoken, firm-minded man. Not
so much in the looks department.

He got some instant coffee from a shelf.

Noah: He came to my island to do some ice fishing one
winter, with a mutual friend.

Me (to Susie): Ask him if he has proof.

Susie: Do you have proof?

Noah: He didn't leave his card, if that's what you mean.

Susie: How can we believe you, then?

Noah: Who's asking you to believe me?

Susie handed the bowl to me.

I sat there with my mouth kind of open but nothing in-
telligent was coming out of it, and I couldn't even spoon any

more beans into it. I put the bowl on the floor. I could hear Hobbes licking at the dregs.

Susie: It—it's just that this is so important to us.

Noah: Girl, there's some things you can't prove. What would prove it? If I had his signature? I coulda bought it somewhere. If I had a picture? You could say I doctored it. Like I said, some things you can't prove. I can tell you about it. Or not. Up to you.

Susie (nodding): Please.

Noah: Welp. He was a nice feller and we got some good fishing done.

We waited. He made coffee for himself, gesturing to Susie with his cup to ask if she wanted some. She shook her head.

Me: And?

Noah babied his fire.

Susie: Did he say anything about—about Calvin?

Hobbes: Did he say anything about Hobbes?

Noah: Sure, it come around to that evench. Wasn't much of a comic reader, myself, but I heard of him, and he chatted about it, brief.

I waited. He took a long, loud slurp of his coffee, then tipped his head slightly to one side and stared into the mug as if he saw something in it.

Susie: So do you think he's sad about Calvin being . . . over?

Noah (shrugging): People say stuff when they're fishing.

He seemed deep in thought while he said it.

Susie: What else? Can you tell us anything else?

Noah: You want me to say something particular, something that will make him seem realer than he was before. But he's just a man, a mediocre fisherman who likes a poem once in a while.

Noah looked up at me.

Noah: He wouldn't think much of you.

Right then I believed that with every cell of my body. I wasn't even angry that he said it—it was like he was stating a fact.

Susie: You are a rude man.

Noah: I have traditional values. A man should protect his woman and not put her in harm's way.

Susie: I am my own woman, thank you. And he just wants to walk across a lake, not live on it all winter long, like some people.

Noah:

Susie: If I were your wife, I would wonder how you could protect me if you were away for months of the year.

Noah: I'm a poet. We need solitude.

Susie: So as long as you make a poem out of it, it's okay to hurt people?

Noah: Art is the pinnacle of human achievement.

Susie: Being a decent human being is the pinnacle of human achievement.

She stood up.

Susie: You're being rude to my boyfriend. And further-more, you're a chauvinist. Make a poem out of that. Thank you for the beans. Come on, Calvin.

She started putting on her parka. I was so stunned by the *boyfriend* word that I couldn't move. I looked at Noah, but I couldn't figure out whether to say I'm sorry, or so there. I didn't know whether I should feel lucky that a girl like Susie would stick up for me, or ashamed that a girl like Susie *had* to stick up for me.

Hobbes: Ashamed.

Me: Huh?

Hobbes: That's the answer to the question. Where's your inner tiger? Didn't you learn a thing all those years we hung out?

Susie had her parka on and Noah was staring at the floor.

Me: Susie, did you just say I was your boyfriend?

She was putting on her mitts like she wanted to poke her fingers through the ends.

Susie: Well, you're my friend, aren't you? And you're a boy, aren't you?

Me: I'm your friend now? Since you haven't hung out with me or hardly spoken to me for over a year, it's been hard to tell.

Susie: I already told you I was sorry. I was lured into the game of peer politics, seduced by the potential of popularity.

Me: That was very alliterative of you.

Susie: And now you have to get over it because—because

I get you in a way nobody else gets you. Come on, Calvin, we've imposed on this man long enough.

Noah: Wait. Please.

We looked at him.

Noah: It's dark out there.

Susie: Calvin, come on.

Noah: And cold.

Me (to Susie): No. He's right. This is messed up, you being out here.

Susie: This is getting old. We've discussed this enough. I'm here. Let's go.

Noah: Wait. I think—I think I just figured it out. You helped me figure it out.

Her arms fell still to her sides.

Susie: You did? We did?

Noah: My wife. Please. Sit down.

Susie sat. Noah looked relieved.

Susie: What did you figure out?

Noah: Seeing what you are willing to do for your friend . . . I have to stop looking for metaphors and look at her. I need to observe her deeply, to make our love real, particular. I have to really get her, the way nobody else gets her. I have to go out of my way for her.

Me:

Susie:

Noah:

Susie: Yeah.

Noah finally looked at me, and when he spoke to me next his voice was mellower.

Noah: You guys stay the night here. Grab a bit of floor.

Me (whispering in the dark): Our parents are freaking out by now. Your parents will be blaming me.

Susie: Your parents will know I'll take care of you.

Me: People might think I hurt you.

Susie: That's a myth. People with mental illness don't hurt any more people than anybody else.

Me: Well, anyway, I promise I'll never hurt you.

Susie: You bet you won't.

Me: Even if you're an alien eating my eyeballs.

Susie: I'm off eyeballs these days. Do you have to say crazy stuff like that?

Me: You know what makes me crazy, Susie? Being crazy, that's what. Try staying sane when everyone treats you like you're insane.

Susie: Okay, Calvin. But you know what? You can't say, youcan'texpectanythingfrommeI'mbroken! And turn around the next minute and say, ohwoeismeeverybodytreatsme-likeI'mbroken! Which one is it? I can treat you the way I really feel, or I can treat you careful.

Me: Real. Just be real.

WE WOKE UP EARLY, FEELING GOOD. NOAH WAS GONE
and the fire was out.

For a minute, Bill, I wondered if Noah had been real. But
then there was this cabin and all his stuff around, and when
I looked in the pan there were a couple of dried-up beans.
He had to be real because if he was, then Susie was, too, and
she had really called me her boyfriend, even if she meant
friendboy.

If Noah wasn't real, all bets were off.

Me: Was Noah real?

Susie: Yes, he was.

Me: Then where is he?

Susie: He probably went to see his wife.

Me: Without saying goodbye?

Susie: It's more romantic that way.

Me: How'd he leave?

Susie: Maybe he had a snowmobile.

Me: Are you real?

Susie (lacing her boots): I'm real.

Me: If you weren't real, you could still say you were.

Susie: Yeah, I guess I could.

Me: You're not helping.

Susie: If I wasn't real, I would pretend to care.

Me: Just say I'm real nine times and I'll believe it.

Susie: If I wasn't real, you could make me do that. Since I am, no.

Me: Good point. But with an imaginative instrument like mine, I'm good at creating figments who are resistant to my commands.

Hobbes: I'm no figment.

Me: Figment.

Hobbes: Humans are doofuses.

We decided Noah wouldn't mind if we made some oatmeal, but we couldn't find any oatmeal. I could have sworn I'd seen some on the shelf the night before. Susie found some canned applesauce. I noticed after we ate it that it had an expiration date about three months old. After breakfast we put on our parkas, packed the sled, and headed off the reef.

The sun was sitting on the flat horizon like a big yellow bowling ball.

Susie: Better check the compass.

Me: Yup—there we go. *C* for Cleveland. Okay, Sooz, Noah said his cabin was twenty-two kilometers from the Canadian shore, which means we were going just under four kilometers an hour. Realistically, that's the best we can do. So. By dark, we have to have covered forty-four kilometers. That means we can be there by lunchtime tomorrow. That's a little later than I told Bill, but hopefully he'll wait.

The lake was this huge lung that breathed. As we walked, I could feel it taut under my boots, a membrane, a diaphragm of ice offended by boots. I looked back once, but I couldn't see Noah's reef anymore.

We made two long parallel gouges in the snow. Between our footprints were the neat straight lines made by the sled runners, and just to the right of my tracks were Hobbes's tracks. It seemed wrong somehow, like leaving footprints on the moon that would never disappear.

The good news was that it was a bit warmer than the day before. Still, the air was white with ice crystals. They didn't fall like snow. They hung suspended, so light they couldn't fall, each one reflecting the snowball sun, all frozen flames. Air like that was hard to breathe. You had to melt it as it went down, you had to extract the H_2 from the O.

By mid-morning we were two blasts of heat and color in the whole white cold world. Hobbes was growling a lot, and when the sled started feeling like I was pulling a duffel bag full of lead, I knew he was taking a ride again. By noon, I realized that keeping the same pace all day was going to be impossible.

———

Calvin the arctic explorer surveys the horizon. It is the same, always the same—flat, white, and without landmarks other than the kind that melt. His beautiful assistant is silent at his side, waiting for her leader to give her orders that she will follow blindly, knowing that a clear line of authority is vital to their survival.

Susie (tromping like she wanted to punch through the ice): This really is the stupidest idea of all the stupid ideas you've ever had, and that's saying a lot. How far do you think we've gone?

I knew we hadn't gone far enough.

Calvin the arctic explorer realizes mutiny is in the ranks. He thinks of ways to distract the ranks.

Me: Are you bored?

Susie: No. Tired. Mad. Not bored.

Me: I would like it if my life were a bit more boring.

Susie: Stick with me.

We were both sucking in some pretty serious oxygen by now, and it was harder to talk, but she walked faster when I could get her going on some rant or other.

Me: Sooz, do you ever think about life?

Susie: Of course I think about life. Especially when I'm dying.

Me: What do you think the good life would look like?

Susie: I don't know. Not having hypothermia in the middle of a massive frozen lake?

Me:

Susie: Okay, I'll play. I mean—I guess get an education, a

good job, get married, buy a house, have a kid or two, travel. I guess.

She said it quiet, like she couldn't believe she was saying it.

Me: I thought maybe you wanted to be, like, a great writer or something.

Susie: How did you remember that?

Me: I remember everything about you.

Susie: Don't tell anyone. I never tell anyone.

Me: Not even the boys you dated?

Susie: No. And stop making it sound like I dated hundreds of boys.

Me: Dozens?

Susie: Three.

Me: Three? In one year?

Susie: Could we stop talking about this now?

Me: Only if you admit that being a writer would be your good life.

Susie: Okay. Maybe. I mean, it would, but that's not the most important thing.

Me: Sounds like it could be important.

Susie: Do you know who Marcel Schwob is?

Me: No. Poor guy.

Susie: Why poor?

Me: Well, his name . . .

Susie: He was a great writer—great. Nobody reads him anymore. How about Isaac Babel? Edward Everett Hale? Theodor Fontane?

Me:

Susie: All great writers who nobody really reads anymore. Defunct. Extinct. Forgotten.

Me:

Susie: There are lots of them. Most of them. That's what happens. A few become part of the canon, and they get read because teachers make you read them. But nobody really cares about the people who wrote the books. I think I'd rather invest my time in the ones who will care, like family and friends. I mean, think of it this way, that's what Bill is doing. He got famous, but he realized what was important. He doesn't even like all the fame and whatnot. He doesn't want anybody in his business. If he died I bet nobody would know.

Me: Don't say that! Of course we would know!

Susie: Bill got fired from his first job. That did something to him. He stopped looking for a job and thought about what he really wanted to do. Sometimes our disappointments can be the best thing that ever happens to us.

Hobbes: Tigers don't do disappointment.

Me: What are you saying? I hope you're not trying to tell me that there's anything good about this whole schizophrenia thing.

Susie: It will make you more compassionate toward the suffering of others.

Me: Ack! Tell me you aren't going to use the platitude torture on me . . .

Susie: What doesn't kill you only makes you stronger.

Me: You're doing it! You're evil!

Susie: Everything happens for a reason.

Me: Stop. I'll do anything you say if you'll stop.

Susie: Keep a stiff upper lip. Good things happen to those who wait. You'll thank me someday . . .

Hobbes: I'd eat her if she weren't so cute.

Me: Hobbes says he would eat you if you weren't so cute.

Susie:

Me: Thank you.

Susie: This is making you really sad. This schizophrenia thing.

Me: Yeah.

We kept walking.

WE WALKED FOR A LONG TIME WITHOUT SAYING anything. I was afraid Susie would vanish any second, but I wasn't making the lake up, or how tired I was. I knew I wasn't making up how badly we needed to keep up our pace if we weren't going to run out of food and water. I could have out-walked her, but I wasn't about to leave behind a delusion like Susie.

I tried to trick her into going a little faster by increasing my pace just a bit, not so as she would notice.

Susie: You sped up just enough so you thought I wouldn't notice.

Me: You noticed.

Susie: I notice everything.

Me: So you can't speed up?

Susie: Oh, I could. Sure I could. But I'm just enjoying myself so much out in this arctic waste, why would I want it to be over fast? Let's just take our time and enjoy things, you know?

Being good at detecting subtle sarcasm, I slowed down to match her pace. I kept talking to keep my mind off the sounds of my boots and my breath and my blistering feet. I talked about how much money we could get if we got a really good picture of South Bay Bessie.

We were so hangdog tired, staring at our boots, we almost ran into a snow goon.

There were dozens of them, standing in perfect military lines, row after row of killer snow goons, facing away from us.

Hobbes growled low.

Me (whispering): You can't kill them.

Susie: What are they?

Me: Snow goons. If you kill them, they multiply.

Susie: Orvil never said anything about this. It's some kind of ice formation. They're glowing!

Me: Psycho-killer snow beings who delight in holding you in their stick arms until your blood freezes . . .

Susie (turning to me): Calvin, they're not alive. They don't have arms. They're just . . . strange . . .

Hobbes: They're lethal.

Spaceman Spiff had crashed on a cold planet, and before him strange sculptures of ice rose from the surface, fluorescent. They were the work of a brutal intelligence, an alien hardened by his existence on such an arctic and unforgiving world. It was a comment on the futility of existence . . .

Maybe the loneliest feeling in the world, Bill, is the

feeling you get when you see something no one else can see, or hear something no one else can hear, or believe something no one else can believe. Maybe that's the worst thing about what I have, that alone feeling, knowing that I can't make anyone really understand about Hobbes.

Me: I'm telling you, they're snow goons.

Susie: Okay. Okay, Calvin. You're scared. What do you want me to do?

She was whispering now, too.

Me: We have to walk around them.

Susie: True.

Me: Quietly, so they don't hear us.

Susie: Okay.

Me: Quietly.

Susie: Okay.

Me: We can't kill them.

We walked around the first one, and I saw it close. It was a glowing pillar reaching straight up into the air out of the ice, like a giant inverted icicle. Some were as high as a two-story building, transparent and gleaming in the sun, as if the lake had bared her teeth.

Me: They're just ice formations.

Susie: I know.

Me: How does the lake do it? Make the ice formations?

Susie stared at the one closest to us like it was Michelangelo's *David*.

Susie: And I wonder how they glow like that. It's scary and pretty at the same time.

Just then a thin thread of liquid water spurted straight up on my left. It started to freeze on the way down.

Hobbes: The lake is spitting at us.

Me: The water must be under pressure there. When the water finds a small hole or crack, it spurts up and makes these things.

Susie: Amazing.

Me: Yeah. And they just keep getting bigger and bigger, until—

Susie: Are they dangerous? I mean, do they weaken the ice? Orvil said something about cracks in the ice . . .

Me: Not as dangerous as snow goons.

Susie: No. Not as.

We both stared at the pillars.

Me: Do you think anybody knows about this besides us?

Susie: Nobody knows.

Me: We know a secret about the lake.

Susie: Yeah.

Me: Don't ever tell anyone.

Susie: I won't.

Me: Besides, maybe we're dreaming this.

Susie: Maybe I'm dreaming you.

Me: And I'm dreaming you.

Susie: That would make me your dream woman.

Me: Nah. I would have dreamed up a supermodel or something—ow!

Can punches be meaningful, Bill? I didn't mind that punch. I grinned and then she grinned and for a second I felt like we'd crossed a line. I stopped grinning and put my hand on her head. Right on the top of her head, and then my hand slipped to her cheek. She stopped grinning and looked down at the ice.

Susie: Don't—don't you kiss me.

Me: Who said I wanted to kiss you?

We walked around the snow goons which were just ice formations.

The snow goons which were just ice formations weren't the danger, Bill.

I was. I was the danger.

I had to protect her from me.

But it was already too late for that. I'd brought her along with me, and it was getting on in the day, and our feet and legs had gone way beyond what feet and legs had evolved to do. I knew we weren't making time like we should, especially not now that we were having to go out of our way to get around the snow goons which were just ice formations.

We kept walking.

IT WAS HALF PAST FOUR WHEN WE HAD TO STOP TO rest and eat dinner because we were starving. Susie sat on the sled. We both knew we were eating the last of our gorp and beef jerky. We had two bottles of water left, some raisins, and two small tubes of peanut butter. That had to be breakfast the next day, our last meal on the ice. I didn't say anything to Susie, but I was guessing we weren't going to be having lunch in the U.S. of A.

Susie: Next to Noah's beans and bread, this is the best food I've eaten.

Me: Hunger is the best sauce.

Hobbes: Give me some.

I dropped some bits of the gorp at my side so Susie wouldn't see.

Susie: How far do you think we are, Calvin? Will it take as long tomorrow as you thought? Maybe we'll make brunch? How far?

Me: Did you know that zebra mussels are killing this lake?

Susie: That far? But you said we'd be there by lunchtime tomorrow. It's going to be dark again soon, and I don't see shore.

Me: Zebra mussels eat all the microbes and make the water nice and clean and clear, but then all those microbes are what the fish eat. The zebra mussel is destroying the entire ecosystem of the lake. One day the whole lake will just be a big tank full of zebra mussels. All thanks to ballast water dumped in the lake by a European boat. I found that out when I was doing avoidance research on my biology project.

Hobbes: That's it? These crumbs are all I get?

Susie: Tell me. I can deal.

Me: And then they'll go on to the next lake and destroy it.

Susie: Wow. You-won't-even-answer-me far?

Me: The largest freshwater lakes in the world and we're slowly turning them into cesspools, flushing our human waste into them, dumping our chemical waste into them, fishing them out faster than the fish can repopulate, tossing in anything we don't want to see anymore—shopping carts, cars . . .

Susie: You're depressing me now, Calvin.

Me: We're basically walking on a big frozen garbage Popsicle.

Susie: Shhh.

Me:

Susie: Thank you.

Me:

Susie:

Me:

Susie: It didn't help.

Me: What didn't help?

Susie: You shutting up—it didn't help. When we started out you told me seventeen hours.

Me: I said seventeen to twenty.

She got the compass out of her pocket.

Susie: I know how to use this thing. I know we're not going in circles.

Me: I wasn't counting on slogging through deep snow in some places, and climbing snow dunes, and going around snow goons. Seventeen hours was at five K an hour. We made four yesterday, but now I'm thinking we're down to three. Maybe.

Hobbes: Hungry . . . hungry . . .

Susie looked so worried sitting there on the sled that I knew I had to say something to make her happy.

Me: So, Susie, I was going to do my biology project on the pollution in the lake. So since I've done all this research, do you think Mr. Ferrige would give me an extension?

Susie (standing): Calvin!

Me: What?

Susie: Yes! That's exactly what you should do. Get an extension!

Me: Why are you suddenly so happy?

Susie: Because! Because you're not giving up! On school, I mean. What a relief! You need a good education . . . Look, all creative people are a bit crazy. But nobody worries about ten hertz as long as you do something great with it.

Me: Okay, so all I have to do is be brilliant or great and I'll be fine. I'll get right on that.

I grabbed the sled and started walking, and Susie kept up.

Susie: Charles Dickens, he thought the characters from his books were literally following him sometimes.

Me: Even better—I'll work on being a genius.

Susie stopped and looked at me.

Susie: But you are a genius already.

Hobbes: Hoo-boy!

Me (laughing):

Susie: What? You are.

Me: Now you're the crazy one. I am not a genius.

Susie: Calvin, I thought you knew.

I was impressed with my delusionary powers. Not only had I conjured up a whole girl, but she was Susie McLean, and she was saying things that were obviously all about making myself feel better about myself.

Hobbes: Why is she talking like that? Maybe she's just mocking you out of revenge for all those snowballs you chucked at her.

Suddenly I could hear whispering. Nothing I could really hear or understand, but I knew the whisperer was there,

South Bay Bessie, or Jenny Greenteeth, or both, just under the ice, just a thin layer of frozen water between me and them. They thought I was one of them.

Me: I don't belong to you.

Susie: What?

Me: I wasn't talking to you.

Susie: I see.

Me: They're under the ice.

Susie: Oh, Calvin.

Me: They're waiting for me.

Susie: Well, they can wait, then. I won't let them have you.

I stopped. I stood still. The wind was in the hollows of my ears, but the voices were gone.

Me: You made them go away, Sooz.

Susie: Okay. Now we know something.

Me: We do?

Susie: Yeah. We do.

I walked a little faster to put distance between me and the whispers, and Susie kept up until she couldn't anymore, and then we went slow until we were beyond exhausted and it was getting dark.

I TRIED TO BE CHEERFUL ABOUT SETTING UP THE TENT before it got really dark.

Me: Okay, we're behind schedule, but after a good sleep we'll go faster. Maybe we will get there in time for lunch.

We untied the tent from the sled.

Me: Remember confidence, Susie. Believing we can do it. We packed that first, right?

She nodded.

Me: Okay, let's see. Let me do my winter camp checklist. Is there wind protection?

Susie sat on the ice as I did a full turn, examining the flat lake for wind protection.

Me: Unfortunately, no. But is the site free of avalanche danger?

I did another 360-degree turn. Susie put her chin on her knees and smiled.

Me: Yes, I can report that we are unlikely to have an avalanche. There's always an upside, right, Sooz? Let's see—reasonably safe from falling trees? Check. Privacy from other campers? Check. I say this is the place!

Susie pointed to a spot about ten feet away.

Susie: I say there would be better.

Me: Yes, I see your point. That would be an excellent spot.

Susie almost laughed and I did laugh, and even though it wasn't funny she really laughed then, and so did I, and we laughed until we had to stop, and then we laughed a bit more.

Susie: That wasn't funny.

We laughed some more.

I started setting up the tent. Susie told me not to look and wandered off to relieve herself.

Hobbes: I'm thirsty.

Me:

Hobbes: I'm thirsty and hungry.

Me: This tent fights back. I'm going to invent a one-button tent one of these days.

Hobbes was pacing back and forth behind me, growling.

Hobbes: I'm thirsty and hungry.

Me: Go hunt something then. Isn't that what tigers do?

Hobbes (a low, rumbling growl): Yes. That is what tigers do.

I could sense him looking in Susie's direction.

Hobbes: Not much to her. Pretty skinny.

I dropped the tent.

Me: Leave her alone.

Hobbes: Hungry—

Me: I'll fight you.

Hobbes (roaring): THIRSTY!

Me: All right! Here! Help yourself!

I poured a water bottle out onto the ice and while he was lapping it up, I threw some raisins onto the ice for him.

I thought Susie's eyes were going to bug out of her head when she saw that empty water bottle, Bill, the same way you would draw three sets of eyeballs when Calvin was scared silly.

Susie: Calvin—!

Me: It was Hobbes.

I sounded pathetic even to me.

Susie: Calvin, what have you done? That was half our water supply! And we don't have that much food left.

Hobbes was purring.

Me: Hobbes was looking at you like he looks at a steak.

Susie: Oh, Calvin.

I hated myself right then, Bill. I hated Hobbes, too, but mostly I hated myself. And then I felt nothing except fatigue.

Me: I'm sorry.

Susie: Me, too.

Me: Hey, we have a bazillion gallons of water right under

our feet! And snow. We have a desert of un-walked-on, un-peed-on snow. We've got a world of water here!

Susie: Calvin, we can't eat snow. It's too cold, it takes too much body heat to melt it. You get hypothermia.

Me: I know that. You think I didn't know that?

Hobbes (chuckling):

Me (to Hobbes): Quiet! This is your fault.

Hobbes: I feel poetic. Tiger, tiger, burning bright / In the frozen of the night, / What immortal hand or eye / Could bake you up a pumpkin pie?

Me: That's not how it goes.

Hobbes: That's the original. Blake ruined it.

Me: Pumpkin pie?

Susie: I'll keep watch over the rest of the raisins and the peanut butter.

We finished setting up the tent in silence.

It would have been better if she'd yelled at me, but she was just quiet. We threw our sleeping bags in and then stood awkwardly outside the tent. I didn't know what to say. Well, are you coming to bed now? It just didn't sound right. Besides, I felt sick looking at the empty water bottle and smushed raisins on the ice. I looked everywhere but there.

Finally I looked up.

Stars.

Millions and bazillions of stars.

Not even stars—galaxies. Galaxies of stars. They filled every little dusky inch of sky, horizon to horizon, with creamy lights.

Me: Susie, look up.

She looked up and gasped.

Susie: It's like we're in a snow globe.

Me: A star globe. If God shook it, all those stars would fall down onto us, like snow.

Hobbes: In what distant deeps or skies / Burnt the fire of thine eyes? / All who see you do admire / And your fur coat do desire.

Me: Blake is rolling in his grave.

Hobbes: He should have asked me for advice.

Me: Right.

Susie: What did you say?

Me: I'm a dot.

Susie:

Me: I'm a dot on a lake, which is a dot on the planet, which is a dot in the galaxy, which is a dot in space. I'm a dot on a dot on a dot on a dot . . .

Susie (staring up): Yeah.

She said it softly, like I'd just said something profound.

Hobbes: Then the stars began to cheer / For the tiger without peer.

Susie: Somehow that sky puts things in perspective.

Hobbes: And what artist and what art / Could make you

play your tiger part? / And when you began to lose some heat, / It made you long for good fresh meat.

Me (to Hobbes): You're killing me.

Susie: I'm going into the tent now.

She went into the tent.

Unbelievably, I went in, too.

Calvin the boy is in a tent with a girl.
A cute girl. A small tent.
Calvin is lying in a small tent with a cute girl.
He and the girl are cold.
He has heard about being cold. In a tent. With a girl.
True, the girl has on a parka and a hat and is in a sleeping bag. But Calvin takes his luck where he can get it.

When I was eleven, Bill, I wondered who came up with the gross idea of taking your germy mouth—the first thing you use in the digestive process—and smashing it up against somebody else's germy mouth, which minutes before could have been masticating slimy avocados or two-month-old fruitcake. Then I turned twelve and it sounded like the most brilliant idea ever invented, as long as it was with Susie. That's what I was thinking about lying there in the tent beside her.

Susie: This is the flimsiest excuse for a tent I've ever seen. This is supposed to protect us from this arctic wasteland?

The wind bucked the sides of the tent and we zipped our sleeping bags up to our chins. It felt amazing to lie down. My legs and feet were singing.

Susie: This thing doesn't want to be a tent, it wants to be a kite.

It was dark, but Susie—she was like this small, pale moon beside me, just a tiny bit shiny, like something was inside her that darkness couldn't put out.

We lay there not talking and my whole body couldn't get over that I was lying in the dark beside Susie. I mean, it couldn't be real, Bill, but it felt as true as anything. Even in a hat she was pretty.

Hobbes: Some tigers might even say she's hot.

We lay there for a while, not saying anything.

Me: I'm sorry for all the times I was mean to you when we were little kids.

She turned toward me. I could feel her looking at me.

Susie: I accept your apology.

But she said it softly. I could tell she was smiling when she said it. You can always hear a smile.

We lay in the dark on the hard ice, and I felt really far away from everything, like my parents and school and Leamington—like I was in space and they were all on a really far planet.

Me: Tell me what you did for your English project.

Susie: You mean the one that's worth 50 percent of your final mark and that you haven't even started?

Me: Yeah. That one.

Susie: I wrote a story. A long story.

Me: What about?

Susie: I'm not saying.

Me: Why?

Susie: You'll laugh at me.

Me: I promise I won't laugh.

Susie: I've fallen for that one before.

Hobbes: She has.

Me: I promise.

Susie: Okay. Let's say it was a novel about friendship and loyalty, and how a young woman comes to define those terms in the context of a difficult relationship—

Me (stifling laughter): A romance? Wow.

Susie: Not a romance! At least, not that kind of romance.

Hobbes: You know nothing about romance. Now, in my experience . . .

Me: How does it end?

Susie: I handed it in with an open ending.

Me: Why?

Susie: I don't know . . . Maybe I just haven't figured out the last chapter yet.

Me: You always finish your homework. I wish I could be like that. I just don't get why I have to learn all that stuff.

Susie: Because if you want to do something new and amazing, you have to know what the world already knows.

Me: Surprisingly that makes some sense. But that means

they have to cram thousands of years of knowledge into the child's developing brain so that by the time it has achieved adulthood it has been initiated into the entire encyclopedic treasury of human knowledge.

Susie: Or maybe just the basics. A taste.

Me: Filled with this knowledge, the maturing generation struggles against enormous odds to discover something new. It faces a unique challenge, bears a great burden. The Change the World Lottery cannot be won.

Susie: Maybe the advances made by our generation will be ethical rather than technological. Maybe our generation will heal the atmosphere and enrich the ethnosphere.

Me: Ethnosphere?

Susie: Yeah. The thin vapor around the earth that is made up of all the dreams and hopes and ideas and imaginations of all the people of all time.

Me: Does it have a hole in it, like the ozone?

Susie: We blow holes in it all the time, but then someone like you comes along and fills it all in again, makes it creamy and fluffy again, like meringue on a pie.

She sort of breathed in sharp after she said that, as if she couldn't believe the words that had come out of her mouth.

Me: See, when you say stuff like that, I know I'm making you up, just like I'm making up Hobbes.

Susie: Maybe we're all making everything up as we go.

Hobbes: Kind of a pie-in-the-sky idea, if you ask me.

Susie: Maybe—

She stopped.

Susie: Maybe this is the last chapter.

Me: Last chapter?

Susie: Of my book, I mean.

Me: Everybody dies?

She made a sound like a fake sigh.

Susie: No—I mean this, you and I—

I didn't dare guess what my delusion was trying to say to me, but I'll tell you something, Bill. Lying there in that tent, I loved her in the front of my brain just as much as in the sides and the back. I wanted to tell her, but even with a sick brain, I knew better than to say it like that, to come up on her quick like that. So instead I worked into it slow.

Me: Did you really call me your boyfriend? Back there at Noah's?

Susie:

Me: Nah—you didn't.

Susie:

Me: Because that would be too weird.

Susie made another exasperated sound.

Susie: Calvin. Don't pretend you don't know about us.

Me: Us?

Susie: Because you know you love me. You've always loved me.

Me:

Susie: And I love you. Deep . . . deep down.

Me: !

Susie: You fell in love with me in first grade and you never wanted anybody else in our life. Don't try to deny it. That's why I kept all those hate valentines, Calvin.

She said it in a way that sounded like she was mad that she'd had to spell it out for me.

Me: Well, that may prove that I love you . . .

Susie:

Me: But it doesn't explain why *you* love *me*.

Susie: Sometimes a thing remains a mystery, a thing that boggles reason, that baffles and strikes wonder in the most logical mind.

Me:

She laughed, and then she looked right through the dark and into the corneas of my eyes and through the irises and all the jelly eyeball stuff and dodged the floaties and focused in on the foveae of my retinas.

Susie: Okay, I'll tell you why I love you, Calvin. But I might only tell you once, so listen up. You have the guts of a tiger, a space explorer, a race car driver, a luge athlete. You have this amazing imagination. You're never boring. You aren't afraid to ask hard questions and find out there aren't any answers. And you—you also know me in a way nobody else knows me.

Suddenly I felt sorry for her, whether she was real or not—for anyone who would love somebody who threw away food and half their water supply to feed his imaginary tiger.

Me: But . . . but you're beautiful . . . and people like you, and I'm . . . you know . . .

Susie: I know about you, but you don't know about you. I bet you didn't know that half the girls at school think you're cute, and funny, and scary smart.

Me: No girls even look at me.

Susie: They're sneaky about it.

Hobbes was laughing somewhere just behind me and to my right, and Susie, the only truly cute girl I've ever met, is telling me to my face she's mine or I'm hers and I'm deciding at that moment that this schizophrenia thing has its upside and I should just go with it.

Me: I kept all the nice valentines I made for you but was too chicken to give you.

Susie: You made nice ones?

Me: Yeah.

Susie: Will you give them to me when we get back?

Hobbes: If you get back.

Me: Yes. I'll give them all to you. Including the one I've already made for Valentine's Day coming up.

Susie:

Me: So—does this mean we get to kiss and stuff?

Hobbes: Only if I can eat your face.

Me: I was talking to Susie, you mangy—

Susie: Well, I don't know . . . schizophrenia . . . it's a bit of a turnoff . . . Yes.

The wind that had been thrashing the sides of the tent suddenly quieted.

Me: I thought you just said yes.

Susie: Have you ever kissed anybody?

Me: Sure. Dozens.

Susie:

Me: No.

Susie: No. And you know why?

Hobbes: Because girls don't want to kiss him.

Me: Because girls don't want to kiss me.

She raised up on her elbow. I could smell her breath, which was like the best smell in the world, like she'd just eaten a breath mint, except I knew she hadn't.

Susie: How do you know girls don't want to kiss you? Have you ever tried?

Me: No. You have to talk to them first. I think that's the rule.

Susie: Right. And you don't talk to girls. And why is that?

Hobbes: He's socially awkward.

Me: I'm socially awkward.

Susie: They don't know that. I know it, but I don't tell them. I let them be intimidated by your silence.

Me: Why?

Susie: Because I wanted to be your first kiss.

Me:

Susie:

Me: Have you ever kissed anyone?

Susie: Of course. I had to practice so that when you finally got around to kissing me, one of us would know what to do.

Me: Always a good idea to plan ahead.

So I kissed her.

I kissed her and she kissed me back so I kept kissing her and she kept kissing me and we kissed and kissed and I wondered if anybody else in the world had ever felt like this because how did they ever stop, and me in my parka and snow pants and hat and her in hers, we couldn't stop. I thought we would burn a hole in the ice.

That kiss felt like the meaning of life.

Me: That kiss felt like the meaning of life.

Susie giggled.

Hobbes: You made her giggle. Yowza!

Me (to Hobbes): Out!

Susie: What?

Me: I'm speaking to Hobbes.

Susie: Stop it or I'll make you cry.

Me: Oh, yeah? Like to see you try.

So she kissed me again, and I swear it did, Bill, I swear it made me cry, and for the first time I knew something my brain could never know, and for the first time I liked that it could ask a bigger question than it or I could answer.

When we stopped to breathe, I opened my eyes and the moonlight and starlight filled up the tent.

Me: Now I understand why a guy can give up his freedom

and shackle himself to one girl and spend the rest of his life working at a job he hates just to support the girl's offspring and then he dies, the end.

Susie: Yeah, and now I understand why a girl can give up her freedom and shackle herself to one guy and ruin her body giving birth to the guy's offspring and put her career on hold and not realize her dreams of travel so she can cook and clean and raise the offspring of the guy and then she dies, the end.

Me: Wow. You win.

I drew her close.

Me: You're real, Susie. Even if you're not, you're the realest thing that's ever happened to me.

WHEN I WOKE UP IN THE MORNING, THE SUN WAS RISING and a warm wind was blowing outside and Susie was looking at me with this Mona Lisa smile on her face.

I jumped up, knowing we had to travel as fast as we could, knowing we didn't have enough food and water for a whole day, knowing it was probably going to take us a whole day, knowing you'd be there, Bill, waiting, wondering, worrying, with that comic strip.

Susie: Good morning, Calvin.

Hobbes: Good morning, Calvin.

Me: Morning.

Susie:

Me: Don't bother rolling up your sleeping bag. We're leaving the stuff behind.

She was staring at me funny.

Me: What? I know it cost money, but maybe we can come back for it with a snowmobile later. The sled is slowing us down, and we've got to get a serious move on. We're leaving it.

Susie: Is that all?

Me: Should there be something else?

Susie: Yes.

Me: What?

Susie: Well, we kissed, you know.

Me: I haven't forgotten.

Susie: You can't kiss me and act like everything is the same.

Me: I'm not acting.

Hobbes: Here we go.

Susie: You have to wake up in the morning and treat me like somebody who has exchanged saliva with you for the first time.

Me: Susie, let me explain: We have to *go*.

Susie: Argh. Never mind.

She sat up and started lacing her boots.

Susie: We kissed.

Why was I so scared to tell her that at the age of seventeen I had just had the happiest event of my life, and it was all downhill from here because Susie McLean had kissed me like she meant it? And how I was scared that it might not be real, or it might not ever happen again because life wasn't meant to be that lucky?

But the expression on her face was the same as she'd had in first grade when I'd called her gross and booger brain. It was the same face I'd thrown snowballs at, and I knew I had to tell her.

Me: Okay, let me explain something to you.

I put my hand on hers so she would stop lacing her boots.

Me: See, Sooz, your brain stem takes care of your biological functions: your heart beating and your lungs breathing. That's the part of your brain that wires you up to mature and produce hormones and so on. Okay, mine did a good job on the hormones, at least. And then there's the R-complex or your reptile brain, and that one is responsible for basic survival. It's aggressive and territorial and drives you to have sex. That part of my brain also works well, to my huge relief. And then there's the limbic system, and that's over your emotions and moods. That's the one that makes you fall in love. That one took care of business when I was in first grade.

Susie (smiling soft):

Me: And then there's the cerebral cortex. The cerebral cortex is the brain that is intuitive and analytical and creative and spiritual. The cerebral cortex is the brain that is responsible for art and science and all the things that make us human. That's the brain that makes you get married in a church and makes you stay in the relationship for sixty years and makes you write poetry to your wife when she's seventy years old. And that, Sooz, is the part of my brain that may be sick but is firing on all cylinders over you right now.

Susie: Your cerebral cortex?

Me: Yup.

Susie: That's the most romantic thing . . . I mean, ditto.

Me: Ditto? I make this whole long speech and you say ditto?

Susie: Okay, let me put it this way: your cerebral cortex is firing up my R-complex.

Me: That sounds interesting.

Susie: Oh, it is, it is.

She stood up.

Susie: But we have to go.

We quickly ate our peanut butter tubes and our raisins, and I kept glancing at her and she kept being there. When we were done she dug in the duffel bag for the compass and pulled something out with a whoop.

Susie: Cookies!

Me: Cookies?

Susie: Thank you, Orvil Watts!

We grinned at each other. Susie checked the compass and we got walking.

It wasn't a white sun, it was orange as tiger fur. The lake ice was rough now, slabs like tumbled blocks, and swells of shattered ice. Soon I was sick of hearing my own breath pumping in my ears.

We were still sore and blistery from the day before, and it just got worse. We put one foot in front of the other until I forgot why I was doing this and where I was and who I was. Hobbes growled a lot. For a long time we didn't talk. We were stuck in that place between hating to move and not having any other option.

Susie checked the compass often.

Susie: What does *S* stand for again?

Me: It's a direction.

Susie: What's a direction?

Directions didn't mean much in the middle of a white-lake nothing.

Orvil was right when he said the lake was a leftover ocean. People who only looked at her from shore, from solid ground, never really knew anything about the vastness of her. She was an immortal being. Immortal beings don't understand mortals. They don't understand what it feels like to know that any given minute might be your last. The lake didn't know what it felt like to be hungry, when your stomach started digesting its own protective lining and your intestines were collapsing in on themselves and your liver and pancreas were puzzled and on standby and all your cellular functions had nothing to function with.

Later in the day the sky was white-blue and the ice was blue-white and it felt like we were in a sensory deprivation cell. We weren't even casting shadows. It was warmer than the day before, a lot warmer, in fact, but the wind never let up, and it sucked the heat and water right out of us. We took sips of water, and I made Susie drink the last bit. I started talking all over the place to keep our minds off it.

Susie: You're scared, aren't you.

Me: Why do you say that?

Susie: Because you're talking a lot. You're trying to keep my mind off things.

Me: Things like what?

Susie: Like I can't feel my feet anymore.

Me: Did you know it *is* possible to find two snowflakes exactly alike?

Susie: No. It's not.

Me: Yes, it is. Of course, the odds of finding twin snowflakes is one in 10^{158}, which is greater than the number of atoms in the universe.

Susie: It's cool to think that odds can be bigger than the universe.

Hobbes: The odds of you making it home alive are bigger than the universe.

Me: Susie, do you believe in God?

Susie: You asked me that before.

Me: Yeah, but that was when I thought he gave us a car.

Susie: You can't believe only when you get stuff.

Me: So are you saying you do?

Susie: Yes.

Me: You do? Really?

Susie: Yes.

Me: Why?

Susie: Don't act like it's so strange—me and three billion other people in the world.

Me: So you believe so you can be part of a club? What about evolution?

Susie: Evolution—maybe that's the way God does it. Maybe God came down every so often and said, Hey Life, Get Complex!

Hobbes: And then he created the tiger and rested from his labors.

Me: There's no God.

Susie: Prove it.

Me: Haven't you heard of Russell's teapot?

Susie: Huh?

Me: This philosopher guy, Bertrand Russell—he said, if I say there's a teapot orbiting the sun somewhere, it's up to me to prove it, not up to the other guy to disprove it.

Susie: So?

Me: So? The teapot? You prove it.

Susie: Of course there's a teapot.

Me:

Susie: Quantum physics, anyone? Infinite number of universes? In one of those universes is a teapot in space.

Me: Is there tea in it?

Susie: Warm, with sugar.

Me: Are there crumpets?

Susie: What's a crumpet?

Me: Something that goes with tea.

Susie: Then there shall be crumpets.

Me: So why doesn't God show himself?

Susie: I don't know—maybe I don't believe enough. Half of me yes, half of me no, but I always speak for the yes side. And I mean, if there *is* a God, it's probably a good idea to believe in him. But if there *isn't* a God, then we're just an accident of nature, a virus, pond scum gone berserk, and it

143

won't matter one way or another if I believe or not because who cares?

Me:

Susie: And so if it doesn't matter, then I choose to believe. There's something mindful about it, about the universe having a heart, us being watched over, maybe life and everything meaning something . . .

Me:

Susie:

Me: I guess I wonder, who is in charge here? Where is the evidence of the Ultimate Grownup? Seems like everyone goes around thinking someone is in charge, and they go through their lives thinking that the higher they get on the mountain, the closer they get to meeting the guru on top. And then one day they get to the top and nobody's there. God could clear up a lot of things if he'd just show up to a meeting at the UN or make a brief appearance at the White House, maybe the Pentagon, Times Square—

Hobbes: Free all the tigers in the zoos . . . !

Me: You'd think somebody who hears a tiger all the time could believe in something other people don't see. But actually it makes it worse. Maybe the first guy who invented God was delusional. Maybe if reality is up for grabs, then there's no Ultimate Reality, which is what God would be in charge of if there was one.

Susie was concentrating, like she was replaying in her mind every word I just said.

Susie: That's the thing, isn't it. Why doesn't he show himself? Course some people say he does—to them—but people don't believe them and they kill them or beat them up or drive them away for saying it, and some people do believe it but use it to make themselves think they're better than anybody else which causes all kinds of problems. God's probably sitting up there smacking his forehead and saying, kids, kids, what'm I gonna do with you?

We walked along without talking for a while, but walking without talking felt desperate and boring and soon all you could think about was the pain in your legs and food and water and sleep.

Me: It will be awesome when Bill shows himself.

Susie: He burned out. You can't do something that consistently brilliant for ten years and not burn out.

Me: No excuse to disappear.

Susie: He knew he'd done his best work. He worked like a madman. He needed a rest.

Me: No reason to deny interviews, not show up for awards, refuse to answer fan mail.

Susie: He rejects fandom. He's modest. Sensible. He knows all that stuff is shallow and pointless.

Me: He's an artist! Art means communication! Why doesn't he communicate?

Susie: Maybe someday he will. Even Lee Salem said that, said Bill hasn't locked the door and thrown away the key. He's just not a sellout, is all. He thinks selling out is buying into someone else's values. Or maybe he knows there's power in creating something and then stepping out of the way. All that silence, that refusal to show up for adulation—it forces you to look harder at the creation itself, like he's saying, this is what I have to say. You laugh, you cry, you think, you change—and that's the point.

We walked in silence for a long time. She was getting slower, breathing harder, but she picked up a little when we talked.

Me: He'll be onshore with the comic strip when we get there. He'll swear us to secrecy, and we'll take it to our graves.

Susie. Okay. How much longer?

Me: Not much.

Susie: Promise?

Me: Promise.

Susie: Calvin, this past year?

Me: Yeah?

Susie: That was the worst part, not having talks about stuff like this.

Me: Yeah. That was the worst for me, too.

SUSIE GAVE ME ONE COOKIE.

Me: You eat mine.

Susie: Why?

Me: I'm rationing.

Susie: I'm the leader of this expedition. I'll say when we're rationing.

Me: All great leaders listen to the rank and file.

Susie: I think you think you don't deserve that cookie.

Me: And you'd be right. You know what's interesting to me about the digestive process? We know empirically that the food in your stomach can be all colors. Like when you throw up you never know what color it's going to be. But you know pretty much what color it's going to be when it comes out the other end. I guess bile does that—makes everything brown. Unless you're a baby. My mom's cousin had a baby and his poop was always surprising. Once he had a game piece in there, the Monopoly iron. Another time he had a Lego. Blue.

Susie was staring at the cookie with a disgusted look on her face.

Susie: I'm eating it anyway, but only if you eat yours. We'll take a bite at the same time.

Slowly we lifted our cookies, staring into each other's eyes. We bit in at the same time, and then stuffed the rest into our mouths as fast as we could.

Lunchtime had come and gone without any lunch except oatmeal cookies, which Susie handed out like hundred-dollar bills. My legs felt like lead prostheses and still no sight of shore. The wind coming from the south was relentless. It never slowed or took a breath.

Susie was taking deep breaths. All I could think about was food.

Me: Did you know I disagree with both individual and world hunger?

Susie: And war.

Me: And war. I bet if we got all the Mensas and all the big moneymakers and all the big technology brains together, and all the artists and musicians and filmmakers, and put them in a room and said, don't come out until you've solved world hunger and war, I bet they could do it. Right, Susie?

Susie nodded.

Me: You have to answer.

Susie: Yeah. I bet, too.

It sounded like yeahh ah beh too because her mouth was as cold and dry as mine was.

Me: Which raises a philosophical question. If I'm against war, how does this impact the decisions I make on a more personal level? Take Maurice. When he acts like a jerk toward me, like some countries do toward others, do I fight back? Isn't that how wars are started? It goes against my principles to lower myself to his level of behavior, but I've tried reasoning with him, I've tried being nice to him, I've tried being a good sport, and things just get worse.

Susie: Why didn't you ever tell me?

Me: You mean why didn't I call on my allies? Should I have involved them in peace negotiations? Do you think that would work?

Susie: No.

Me: We'd have to impose sanctions. Like you could refuse to talk to him, refuse to let him throw his arm around you as you're walking down the hall, for example. Not share my sandwich with him.

Susie: That was your sandwich?

Me: It's always my sandwich. He doesn't share his own.

Susie: Hmm . . . You could just punch him in the nose.

Me: Maybe it's the uneven distribution of resources that causes the problems.

Hobbes: You unevenly distributed your peanut butter.

Me: So stupid how some people have four toilets and some people have none, how NBA players get a new pair of shoes for every other game while some kids go their whole lives without a single pair. Right, Susie?

Susie: Right.

She said right without the *t* on the end of it.

Me: And what is it about balls anyway? Find a person who can hit a ball really well with a stick or put one through a hoop or knock one into a little hole in the ground, and we pay them bazillions of dollars. Seriously, people, it's a ball. A toy! Huh, Susie? What if we gave all that money to the poor people, set them up in business or something?

Susie: Toy . . .

Me: And how idiotic is it that some even pretty ordinary people over here have a single house as big as a whole African village, for only two people and their kid-dog. Really? Really? And these are supposedly sane people, Susie. You know what's even stupider, Susie—even stupider than all that? That we all sit around and let it happen.

Susie (with a dreamy smile): That's why I picked you.

Me: That's a good answer, Susie. More than one word is good. Did you know the last war cost three trillion dollars? What if we got together over pizza and said, here's three trillion dollars. We can use it to kill people, or we can use it to solve our differences. I bet three trillion dollars could go a long way toward solving a few differences. I bet our best TV-commercial makers could help people understand how moronic war is. What do you say to that, Susie?

Susie: Mmmm . . .

Me: That's not a word.

Susie: Moronic.

Me: Okay, okay, because that was three syllables. It's just that the world is so big, Susie. We think we can't change anything because if we tried someone would call us crazy, but I can tell you that that is not the worst thing in the world.

I thought about what I'd just said for a minute.

Me: Okay, maybe it's up there, but not the worst thing—

Hobbes: Look at her. She's cold, she's exhausted. Her lips are chapped—

Me: Susie—Susie, you doing okay?

Susie: I really can't feel my feet. How much longer, Calvin?

I took off my mitten and scooped some snow in my bare hand. I held it until it melted.

Me: Here, Susie.

She lifted my cupped hand to her lips and slurped like a cat.

I did it again.

I did it until my hand was too cold to melt the snow.

Susie: So good.

Me: You're doing great, Sooz. You're strong.

Susie: Not strong. Tell me again why we had to do this?

Me: I don't know.

Susie:

Me: I don't know anymore.

Susie:

Me: I—I think I was trying to understand, trying to

figure out why I am the way I am. I think I felt like if Bill came out and made a comic about me, I'd understand something about myself, just like Scout did when Boo Radley came out. It would make me feel like the broken bits of me were put back together and the cracks might even disappear—

Hobbes: Crack.

Me:

Hobbes: Crack in the ice.

I looked. A crack in the ice.

Me: Just step over it.

Hobbes: You step over it.

I stepped over the crack.

I lived.

The ice felt firm under my feet, but soon I saw another crack, and then another.

Susie: The ice is breaking.

Me: No. Remember what Orvil said. These are old cracks. It's frozen over again. And the cracks don't intersect.

WE WALKED.

Susie handed out a cookie when we couldn't stand it anymore.

We walked.

Susie handed out the last cookie.

We walked.

Calvin the abominable snowman, yeti for short, surveys his icy kingdom—

Me (to me): Stop it.

Man has driven him into the coldest wastelands—

Me (to me): Stop it, stop it.

His mate, smaller and weaker than him, has been pushed past her endurance. She's a little on the toothy side, and has a tendency to bite, but when you're an extinct race, you take your love where you can.

Me: Doing okay, Susie?

She shook her head.

Me: Let me carry you for a while.

She shook her head again.

Me: Yes, let me carry you for a while.

Susie: I'm too heavy.

Me: Argue not, mate, only obey.

She held out a hand to ward me off.

Susie: Who are you now?

Me: Yeti. We can do this, Susie. Think of it as a video game, and the snow and the cold are the enemy, and all we have to do is get to that next drift of snow, or that bump shaped like a fin, or step on twenty dents in the ice, and we get to the next level. Every level is a bit harder than the one before, but if you avoid trapdoors and keep moving around, you're good. You're sort of good.

She shook her head. She didn't want to play.

Me: Susie, when we get to the other side of this lake, I'm going to buy you fried eggs and lots of white-bread toast slathered in real butter, with pancakes for dessert.

Susie: And a breakfast brownie.

It sounded like bre-fash bow-nee.

Me: There's no such thing as a breakfast brownie.

Hobbes: There should be.

Spaceman Spiff looks out over the frozen wasteland of Planet Erie. It has been well named, he thinks wryly. He and his fellow astronaut are doomed, of course, stranded as they are on this cold ball of rock and ice, hurtling through the blackness of space. They have contacted the father ship. All hope is not lost. But did the captain get the message? Will he think it worth it to interrupt his own mission to rescue them? They will be declared heroes for the cause of space exploration, and people will speculate about how long it took them to die.

But Spiff doesn't give up that easily. Eventually the father ship will come to this planet, and won't the captain be surprised to find they have conquered the elements and survived against all odds. Spiff looks at his female sub-officer. She is a good astronaut— uncomplaining, forging ahead in the hopes of finding shelter. Wouldn't the captain be surprised to find they had not only survived, but procreated—their firstborn the first citizen of Planet Erie . . .

Susie: Why are you looking at me like that?

Wye r oo lookin ah meh like tha?

Me: Oh, nothing.

Bill, I wanted to live, and most of all I wanted Susie to live, and that's what I was thinking about when I heard the most horrible sound in the world: the sound of Susie crying.

Me: Susie?

Susie (sniff):

Me: Susie?

Susie: Are you kidding me?

Ah oo ki-ing me?

Susie: Where is the shore? We should be able to see the land by now. We're going to die out here on this horrible lake!

Me: Well, the lake itself isn't horrible—

Susie: Don't you talk to me!

Me: I just—

Susie: Don't! Don't you talk to me ever again! I'm not speaking to you, you understand? Ever, ever again. That's what you get for killing me.

Me: Susie, I'm not going to let you die.

Susie: Let me? *Let me?* I'll tell you what, you don't *let me* do anything. I don't need your permission to do anything, including dying.

Me:

Susie (gasping a little):

Me: Is there a correct response to what you just said?

She stood still.

Susie: I can't move now.

I put my arms around her.

Yeti's mate laid her head on his shoulder and some primeval feeling he could not articulate filled his being. He would do this. He would get her to safety, to the civilization of man.

It was all his fault, after all.

All his fault all his fault all his fault—

WE WEREN'T FREEZING WITH ALL OUR JUICES IN US.
We were freeze-drying, freeze-squeezing. The lake was
squeezing all the life out of us. I melted more water with my
hands, but it only gave her a slurp or two. My hands were big
toothaches, throbbing.

Hobbes: My paws hurt. I'm thirsty.

When you are in the middle of a flat, frozen lake, Bill, it
looks like you are in the exact center of a perfect circle. Which
is awesome in a way because it's like the world really does
revolve around you, like you're at the center of all meaning.
But then it gets kind of freaky, because no matter how long
and hard you move, you can't get out of the middle of that
circle. No matter where you are, you're at the epicenter of
the known universe, and it follows you wherever you go,
even if it's the stupidest universe you could come up with.

Hobbes: I'm hungry. My paws hurt.

The sun was getting lower on the horizon again. My legs
were setting, too. Soon it would be night and that would

be it for my legs. Susie took slow, shuffling steps. I was colder again.

Suddenly she stopped and shrieked.

Susie: Calvin! Lights!

I almost tripped over my dead feet.

Maybe they were stars . . .

But no, they were lights, distant and tiny, but lights for sure.

Susie: Land! We made it! I thought we were going to die.

I knew things looked a lot closer than they really were on the lake, but I didn't say anything.

Susie: Oh.

Me: Oh?

She whimpered.

Susie: I think I peed my snow pants.

Me: Okay. It's okay, Susie.

Susie: I didn't mean to.

Me: Yeah, it would be different if you meant to.

Susie: It was warm for a minute.

Hobbes: Can we not go into the details?

Susie: But now it's cold.

And then, Bill, she started shivering.

She was shivering, and every Boy Scout there ever was knew that was bad.

You couldn't escape the reality of shivering.

And right then, Bill, Hobbes walked into my full view—a massive eight-foot tiger with a head the size of a basketball and paws the size of cereal bowls and all his muscles rumbling and popping under his fur. I could see every bit of him now, orange against the white ice and snow and a black Rorschach test on his head. He was as real as Susie, or maybe Susie was as real as him, or maybe nothing was real including me, and I turned slowly around in a circle and came back to Hobbes and Susie, who had sat down.

Me: No, Susie, you can't sit down.

Susie: I'm sleepy.

Me: No. No sleep.

Susie (so softly I could barely hear her): Is this what it feels like to lose your mind, Calvin? Like your brain is filled with a hundred thoughts at once and none of them go together and you don't know if what you're seeing and hearing is for sure? Is that what it's like?

Me: Yeah, Susie. A lot like that. Come on.

I pulled her to her feet, but her knees started bending.

Susie: I'm sorry, Calvin, I can't.

Me: I'll carry you.

Susie: No. I have to walk.

Me: Yeah. You do. Come on.

Susie: In a minute.

She folded down.

Hobbes: Make her mad.

Me: Go away.

Hobbes: Make her chase you.

Me: I—

I stopped.

I bent down and picked up a handful of snow and chucked it at her.

Hobbes: That's it!

Thwap!

Susie: Calvin!

She tried to scream it, but only this shrill pathetic sound came out.

I hit her with another one.

Thwap!

Hobbes: That'll get her up!

Susie: Calvin, what are you doing? Stop it, you freak!

She had put consonants on the ends of all her words.

Me: Snowball fight! Snowball fight! Whoever wins gets to be the boss.

Susie: You do that again, and I'll—

Me: You'll what? You'll what?

I chucked another snowball. *Thwap!*

She stood up like an old woman and picked up some snow and slowly formed it into a snowball.

Susie: This!

I tried to dance around a bit, but I was so stiff I moved like a robot.

Susie: This is for bringing me on this stupid frozen lake—

I dodged and the snowball sailed past me. She bent down again.

Her pitch came faster this time and it caught my leg.

Thwap! I got her again.

Me: You'll have to chase me!

She made a huge snowball.

I plodded in the direction of the lights. She started to stumble after me. She waddled like a baby in a big swollen diaper. We both half screamed and half laughed this dry wheezy laugh, and then I slipped and fell on my backside and she threw the snowball right in my face and said I'm going to pummel you, you jerk, and she swung her arms at me for a while and I held her off at arm's length and then she stopped and breathed hard a minute and finally she said let's go.

I thought we could do it, Bill. Maybe the lights weren't all that far away.

It turns out they were.

THE WIND HAD BLOWN THE ICE BARE AHEAD OF US, SO the going was a bit easier for a while. Then Susie started shivering again.

Hobbes was padding along just ahead of us, not speaking, not looking back at us, and I could see all of him now, all the time. He slunk and weaved in front of me, putting his nose to the ice as if he smelled something under there.

Me: I figured something out, Hobbes. You might always be true about me. I can't control you, I can't make you go away. But you know what? If I can't control you, you can't control me either. That's all I need to know.

Hobbes: You, me, me, you. You can't separate us. Listen to me. Maybe lots of people have a tiger, but they don't know about it. I can help you.

Me: I never wanted to hurt her.

Susie: Calvin, what? What?

Her voice was small and dry, like her throat had almost closed up.

Her face was really peaceful.

Susie: Calvin, I'm so sleepy . . .

She stopped and stood there with her eyes closed.

I picked her up and slung her arm around my shoulders, and she wasn't even heavy, not even a bit heavy.

Me: Don't disappear on me, Susie. Just stay awake, okay, Susie? Even if I can only have the dream of you, I'll take it.

She didn't answer.

And that's when Jenny Greenteeth crawled out.

First her hands, Bill, big and purple with long curly fingernails. Then her head with kelp for hair and fish eyes for eyes, lidless and glassy, and inside her black mouth her teeth furred with green moss.

Hobbes growled.

She crawled out, big and whole.

Jenny: I drowned, but I forgot to die.

Stupendous Man carried the helpless damsel, Susie, in his impossibly muscular arms. If she knew he thought of her as a helpless damsel . . . He walked away from Jenny Greenteeth, but he could hear her following, hear her sloshing along behind him, slosh, slosh, slosh, her dripping skirts dragging on the ice. She kept up with him. She wasn't going to go away. Stupendous Man was going to have to turn around and face her.

Me: Can't we work this out? Can you please just leave us alone?

Jenny: It's warm under the water. Come down.

Me: No, thank you.

Jenny: Why is there a tiger?

Me: Why is there a ghost?

Jenny: I died.

Me: I'm sorry to hear that.

Jenny: The girl is dying.

Me: No.

Jenny: She'll be warmer under the water.

She followed us, but she didn't come any closer, keeping her ice-rimmed eyes on Hobbes. Her eyes clicked when she blinked.

Click. Click.

Jenny: First you're cold, and then you're not cold, and then you're warm and you dream—

Me: You're not real. You're not here. Leave us alone.

Jenny: I'm true.

Me: You're not. I'm making you up.

Jenny: Yes, you made me. I'm made. I'm here.

Me: You have to go now.

The lake was a big drum and the drum was thumping and booming and vibrating at a register just below hearing.

Stupendous Man kept walking, the damsel in his arms. The ice had started to crack behind him . . . Stop stop stop.

Jenny: Lots of monsters under the ice.

Click.

Me:

Jenny: What happened to you?

Click. Click.

Me:

Jenny: Lots of monsters under the ice.

Stupendous Man put the damsel down. Even with his unspeakable strength, he couldn't carry his whole world in his arms forever.

Me: Hobbes! Who's stronger? You or Jenny?

Hobbes: Me. I was always going to save you.

Me: I know.

Hobbes: That was always the point.

Me: Yeah.

Hobbes: We're buddies, right? I know where the ice is good. Just follow me.

Me: Between you and Jenny Greenteeth, Hobbes—who's stronger?

Hobbes: Not much to her.

Me: Please, Hobbes.

Slowly Hobbes turned toward Jenny. He growled and leaped away behind me. I lifted Susie up again and walked.

I could hear Hobbes snarling.

Me: Lots of monsters under the ice, Susie. But that's okay—Hobbes can take care of them.

Susie: Mmm . . .

I heard an unearthly screeching sound, like metal grinding on metal.

Susie: Wassat . . . ?

Me: You heard that, Susie?

Jenny Greenteeth wailed and Hobbes roared and it echoed over the empty lake.

Jenny glubbed and Hobbes yowled. It filled up the whole sky, that yowl.

Susie: The ice is breaking up—

Me: No, Susie, that's Hobbes driving Jenny back down under the ice.

Susie: That's the ice screaming.

Then Hobbes was in front of us again, licking his chops covered in green sauce.

Hobbes: Like I said, not much to her.

And then I put Susie on her feet, Bill, and we stood beside each other and stared at the lights on the shore and I couldn't remember if they were stars or if they were some other thing my mind was inventing, and Hobbes stood with me, and I loved him, and Susie, too, and I cried because I loved me, too, and I'd forgotten that, if I'd ever known it, forgotten, just like I'd forgotten if they were stars or lights.

Then Susie went down.

SUSIE WAS LYING BESIDE ME, CURLED ON THE ICE LIKE a baby, like the lake had a baby and just left it there, not even in a basket or on a doorstep, just left its blue baby there sleeping. I saw cracks in the ice, and this time they weren't going away.

Where were you, Bill? That's what I kept thinking: Where are you? You would have known we were late, really late. I didn't remember being mad since I was six years old, but right then I was so mad I stood up and started shouting—at the lake, at the sky, at you, Bill. Especially you.

Me: Why all the secrecy? All the mystery? Why don't you show yourself? Why don't you answer fan mail? Would it hurt once in a while? Here's a news flash: you're famous! Your creations inspire lifelong loyalty! It's too late! Why couldn't you have cared enough to worry about us, to be here?

I sat down on the ice beside her. The sun was almost sitting on the lake, and it was getting cold again, but I couldn't carry Susie anymore, and I couldn't leave her.

Then Hobbes sat beside us like a big furry furnace, and I felt warm. I felt warm except for my face where my tears were turning into slush. Sitting there, I realized something important, Bill.

You did care.

I knew you cared because you made Calvin for the world with this amazing brain that he could do amazing stuff with. It was like his imagination could look into the Great Bloodshot Eye of Reality and say, wanna fight? It was like his imagination could walk right up to the Golden Throne of Reality and refuse to bow. You made him that way, and if that didn't show you cared, I didn't know what would.

I loved my brain right then, Bill. Even a sick brain was a miracle when you thought about it. Time might be a dimension, but the human brain could chop it up into minute bits, observe it as a phenomenon of existence. Physics and chemistry weren't much without biology and the human brain to guess endlessly about what it all meant. Space might be infinite and full of an unspeakable number of stars, but it didn't know how beautiful it was. I knew. Calvin knew. Calvin of the unbegun English project, Calvin of the unfinished science project, Calvin the schizophrenic maladaptive daydreamer.

I made Susie sit up so I could tell her what I had figured out, but her head was slumpy and loose.

Susie (mumbling): I forget.

Me: What? What do you forget?

Susie: Why living is important.

Me: Well, there's Christmas, Susie.

Susie: Christmas.

Me: And hot chocolate.

Susie:

Me: And comic books.

Susie: And snow.

Me: And summer holidays.

Susie: And kissing.

Me: Best of all.

I kissed her, right on her chapped mouth.

Susie: I can't feel it.

Me: Me neither. But you know what? My amazing brain invented Susie the Figment, who looks exactly like Susie McLean, to come along with me on this hike. And if my brain can do that, it can invent you feeling strong and walking. You're going to get up right now and—

Susie: I can hear a helicopter.

Me: Or it can invent a helicopter—but there is no helicopter. It's the ice groaning . . .

But then there was a helicopter.

It just kept flying toward us from the south. It kept being real, real and big and loud, and it had lights, and it was a helicopter. I stood up and waved my arms and the flashlight and screamed.

Finally it hovered over me like a gigantic monster dragonfly, and I saw them heave a basket out of the opening.

And just then the ice to my right cracked open like a broken skull.

ANOTHER VEIN OF BLACK WATER OPENED UP TO MY LEFT.

Pretty quick we were going to be on an island of ice.

The wind from the propellers beat down on us, but Susie kept staring up, blinking from the wind blowing into her face. Hobbes's fur was blowing in every direction.

A man in uniform had launched himself in the basket and was being lowered toward us.

Paramedic (shouting over the noise of the helicopter): I'm taking her first!

Me: Her?

Paramedic: Pick her up . . .

Me: You see her? Yes, take her! Here she is! You see her!

I picked up Susie in my arms and put my mouth in her hair next to her ear and said, you're gonna be okay now, Susie, you're gonna be okay.

He took her out of my arms like a big rag doll and stuffed her into the basket. Then he crawled in after her and the basket started to lift.

Paramedic: I'll come back for you!

The cracks were slowly reaching around me and Hobbes. The roaring of the helicopter and the screaming and groaning of the ice were deafening and the cracks were widening.

The lake was in my brain. I put that vast lake into my brain, and I could zoom out and see it as a blue splotch on the big ball of the world, or I could zoom in and see each snowflake as a 10^{158} possibility. I was standing on the lake and tucking the corners of it into my skull, but the lake didn't know me. It didn't feel me. It couldn't understand me, zoom in or out on me.

I might be tipping into a cold lake in a minute, but I could imagine a tiger, and a dinosaur based on bones, and monsters under the bed, and I could imagine flying. That's what a sick brain could do—it could know it was sick, it could know it might die. That was the Calvin brain, the human brain. Only the human brain could know about a hot tiger on a cold lake.

I had the lake in me, Bill. But the lake didn't have me.

Not yet.

The basket was coming down for me.

Hobbes: As long as you know—

Me: What?

Hobbes: As long as you know you have a tiger. Don't make me come out. Keep me in.

I nodded, not exactly sure what he meant, but knowing

I could figure it out so long as that basket got down to us in time.

Hobbes: We're buddies.

Me: Yeah.

Hobbes: We're friends.

Me: Yeah.

Hobbes: Don't give up on the Lottery.

Me: Okay.

Hobbes: Don't give up.

Me: I won't.

Hobbes: Don't let Maurice push you around.

Me: Okay.

Hobbes: Remember there's a tiger in you.

Me: Okay.

Hobbes: Do your homework but don't stop having fun.

Me: Okay. Hobbes . . .

The ice floe was tipping and he was grinning his Cheshire cat grin.

Me: Calvin without Hobbes, it just wouldn't have worked.

Suddenly the basket was there and the paramedic was manhandling me into it.

Me: Hobbes! Get in!

Paramedic: Settle down, kid. I've got you.

Me: You have to get Hobbes . . . !

Paramedic: You're really cold. Come on, settle down, or you're going to cause trouble for both of us.

Me: Hobbes!

The basket lifted off and we were high over the ice and then we were in the helicopter.

As we pulled away, I could see Hobbes like an orange blanket floating in the black water.

THAT'S THE WAY THINGS WENT, BILL.

The paramedic who was looking after Susie had started an IV.

Me: Is she going to be okay?

Paramedic 1 (busy):

Paramedic 2 (to me): I want you to wrap yourself in this blanket and hold this heat pack to your abdomen.

Me: But is she going to be okay?

Susie: Where's Calvin?

Paramedic 1: He's here. You can talk to him in a minute.

Susie: Where? I can't see him.

The paramedic gave me a look that said, I have no idea why she wants you but she does, so get your skinny rear over here.

Me: I'm here, Susie.

I knelt beside the stretcher and touched her hair. It was the realest, truest hair I will ever touch.

Susie: Do you think this will make the papers?

Her voice was so small I had to read her lips.

Me: I hope not. I don't want Bill to know what I did to you.

Even while I was saying that, I knew I'd have to tell you everything, confess everything, apologize for everything.

Susie: You owe me. Big-time.

Me: I owe you for the rest of my life.

Susie: Yeah.

She smiled.

I held her hand and had this vision of owing her for the rest of my life, and me old and still owing her.

Me: Okay. Where should I start?

Susie: Take your meds.

I nodded.

Susie: And stick with me.

Me: I'm sticking.

Susie:

Me: Hobbes is gone.

Susie: Is it hard?

Me: It's hard.

Paramedic 2: Okay, kid, I need you to wrap up and put this heat pack—

Me (to paramedic 2): How did you know we were here? Out on the lake?

Paramedic 2: We got a call. All you need to know is that you'll be paying for this little rescue mission until you're well into your thirties.

SUSIE MADE ME GO BACK TO SCHOOL. OF COURSE.

Maurice said the freak is back when I walked in, but everyone else was like, saw you in the paper!

Most said stuff like

what was the helicopter like?

is it true that you and McLean are a thing?

she says you guys slept in the same tent

why are your faces sunburned?

is it true her baby toes froze off?

is it true your toes turn black before they fall off?

I had never been so popular. I thought they would call
me schizo or something, but if they did it wasn't to my
face. Besides, it didn't seem like a bad name anymore. Just
a fact. Sooz and I sat together at lunch the first day back
and Maurice tried to grab my lunch but I stopped him and
Susie told him to go clip his nose hairs so he grabbed her
lunch and I socked him.

He told the principal I was bullying him and I got in

trouble, but Maurice hasn't bothered me since. I have initiated an appeasement policy and hope to find a diplomatic resolution to our ongoing tensions.

My English teacher turned out to be a friendly alien and suggested I write all this down for my English project, and, given the special circumstances, she wouldn't even take marks off for being late. Maybe she was just being nice because I'm onto her about the whole alien thing, but when she sees how many pages it is, maybe she might give me a decent mark.

I also got an extension for my biology project, an essay about how we're polluting and destroying Lake Erie and how the other Great Lakes will be next. Susie read it and said if I don't get an A, no one will.

I got on medication and it helps. It helps a lot, and I don't get any of the side effects. Turns out Dr. Filburn didn't go to school for twelve years for nothing.

I visited soldier guy in the hospital. He didn't salute me this time because he's on meds now, too. Turns out we both like chess. He might be becoming my first guy friend.

Sometimes I can feel Hobbes in the room, or beside me when the fire is going and I'm sipping hot chocolate with marshmallows. I don't mind. I mean, a comic strip called just *Calvin*? It wouldn't have flown.

Hobbes doesn't talk, but feeling him around reminds me not to give up on the Lottery and to make sure I take care of myself.

Our parents thought Susie and I had run away together. Naturally Susie's parents gave me grief about hanging out with her at first, especially when they knew everything that had happened. But she told them we were Calvin and Susie and that's just the way it was. After I had groveled sufficiently they didn't hate me anymore.

Susie makes me do my homework every night and it turns out that if you do that, school isn't as horrible. Susie says get used to it because I'll be going to university for a long time so I can become a neuroscientist. Once I complained about not knowing birds, and she said let me introduce you to the joys of reading and bought me a book on birds. If I ever don't want to do my homework, she starts taking off her shoes and socks so I can see where her baby toes aren't there anymore and I tell her, stop I'll do whatever you want.

Well, Bill.

That's the story.

I'm okay now, even though my brain will be burping up Lake Erie for a long time. I know you didn't create me. You can't make me better and you don't control my destiny. I control me, and I can ask bigger questions than my brain can answer. It's scary to think about that, but it's also part of the adventure. I like to think of you out there doing new and amazing things with your brain.

And this is the second reason I'm writing you this letter: to say thanks. I never found out who told the emergency services to come for us. Apparently 911 callers do not have to give any personal information. Susie and I decided it could have been the cabdriver, or Orvil Watts, or the guy in the doorless truck who was looking for Fred, or Noah.

But why would any of those guys not want to identify themselves?

It must have been you, Bill.

You said yourself the world is a magical place.

Yours truly,
Calvin

ACKNOWLEDGMENTS

My sincere gratitude to

Brenda Bowen
Valerie Battrum
Haley Latta
Patrick Downes
Candace Fisher
Sarah Gough
Asher Mason
Derek Bates
Katie Bates
Dallas Leavitt
Shawna Cordara
Dave Voelker
Margaret Ferguson
Shelley Tanaka
Alberta Foundation for the Arts
Canada Council for the Arts

—M.L.